WANDERING SOULS

AND OTHER STORIES

PHILIP CAPUTO

Arcade Publishing • New York

Arcade Publishing books may be purchased in bulk at special discounts for sales promotion, corporate gifts, fund-raising, or educational purposes. Special editions can also be created to specifications. For details, contact the Special Sales Department, Arcade Publishing, 307 West 36th Street, 11th Floor, New York, NY 10018 or arcade@skyhorsepublishing.com.

Arcade Publishing® is a registered trademark of Skyhorse Publishing, Inc.®, a Delaware corporation.

Visit our website at www.arcadepub.com.
Please follow our publisher Tony Lyons on Instagram @tonylyonsisuncertain

10 9 8 7 6 5 4 3 2 1

Library of Congress Cataloging-in-Publication Data is available on file.

Cover design by Erin Seaward-Hiatt

Print ISBN: 978-1-64821-158-4
Ebook ISBN: 978-1-64821-159-1

Printed in the United States of America

Contents

WANDERING SOULS

Alone in the house—Delia was out meeting with her book group—I'd been watching a *60 Minutes* segment about POWs and MIAs. Anderson Cooper was interviewing a New Jersey woman from Riverside, Barbara Lindstrom, still grieving for her older brother, killed in action in 1969, his remains never recovered. His name, Paul Salerno, didn't register for two or three seconds—forty years had gone by—but when it did, goosebumps scampered up my neck and across my scalp.

"When I think about him—his body lying out there in a jungle ten-thousand miles away—it tortures me to this day," Barbara told Cooper. "It tortured our parents all their lives. Now they're gone." She and Paul had been very close, she went on. Closer than most brothers and sisters. Now and then, he appeared to her in a dream, the same dream over and over: He was in an enclosure that looked like a jail cell, and though he didn't utter a sound, she sensed that he was pleading with her to set him free. The resemblance between the image in her dream and what I'd seen with my own eyes was uncanny.

When the segment ended, I went into my attic, opened a footlocker with my name and army serial number stenciled on its lid, and found the notebook under a pile of musty uniforms. It was in a plastic case. I thumbed through the pages and found the one I was looking for, stained by mildew, but the names and map coordinates still legible.

Why not? I thought. I had the time, an abundance of time, having taken early retirement from the hospital where I'd been a CT and X-ray technician. Then, dwelling on Barbara Lindstrom's anguish, a wave of shame washed over me, and *why not?* hardened into *you must.*

I was the one who'd spotted them under a banyan tree, slumped against the trunk, facing out through the mazed prop roots like captives in a cage.

Our squad had been on patrol when we stumbled across the bodies of three Americans, lying on the trail in a row, all shot multiple times. Ambushed, we figured, and hadn't had a chance to return fire; we found no brass anywhere near them. They wore bush hats instead of helmets and camouflage uniforms without flak vests or unit patches, indicating they belonged to some sneaky reconnaissance-commando outfit, which might have explained why no one told us another unit was operating in the area. They hadn't been sneaky enough, it seemed. Their rifles and magazines were missing, probably taken by the men who'd killed them. With bandannas covering our mouths and noses, we wrapped them in their ponchos. This wasn't easy; they'd been dead at least a day and a night and were stiff as stone statues. The stench made our eyes water, it seemed to burn our skin, an invisible methane flame.

The squad leader, Sergeant Sanchez, split us up into two-man teams and told us to check the area for more KIAs, or—which was very doubtful—any wounded survivors. I teamed up with him. We moved off-trail through a towering jungle canopied by branches woven like a basket. The banyan caught my eye, at first because it was so huge, with its long, thick, horizontal branches dripping aerial roots that sunk deep into the ground to form a kind of fairyland of chambers and alcoves and dim little nooks. And in one of those nooks, I saw something that didn't look like it belonged there. I tapped Sanchez on the shoulder and pointed and we crept up to the tree, cautiously, for a closer look.

"What the fuck, I mean, like, what the fuck?" he said.

Two men, bloated and blue, sat side by side in the shadowed space. Dried blood darkened their uniforms, the same as the ones worn by the dead on the trail. One—the one on the left—had been shot though the chest, the other in the head. A good part of it had been blown away; his own mother would not have recognized him. Sanchez indulged in some forensics, speculating that the pair had survived the ambush, fled into the forest, and somehow squeezed into the cell-like enclosure, maybe to make a last stand (to put a heroic spin on things) but more likely to hide. The enemy must have spotted them, just as I had, and sprayed them with rifle fire. I made sure not to think about what it had been like to die that way, trapped in what they must have hoped would be a refuge.

Sanchez frowned, looking at the roots, some as big around as a man's leg. The corpses would be as rigid as the others; no way we could snake in there and pull them out of that maze, the sergeant said. No way we would *want* to, even if it were possible; in that cramped space, we would be forced into an appalling intimacy with their decomposing flesh.

"Somebody's gonna have to come in with chain saws or axes and cut them out," he said.

He borrowed a pair of latex gloves from me—I was the squad medic—kneeled down, and extending his arm full length, reached in and tore their dog tags from their necks, turning his face aside against the smell. He removed the green tape from the tags—taped to prevent rattling—and read the names and serial numbers and map coordinates to me, which I recorded in my notebook. That was how I learned the identities of the two men: Noel Chandler and Paul Salerno.

Sanchez radioed the company commander, reported what we'd found, and requested a medevac and a chain saw to extricate the men entombed in the banyan tree. Soon, a chopper landed in a clearing nearby, but there was no chain saw on board, no axe, no nothing. We loaded the three KIAs found earlier, climbed in, and flew out, relieved to be out of there. Sergeant Sanchez entrusted our C.O. with the dog tags, explaining why there were no remains to go with them. I read him the map coordinates of where we'd found Chandler and Salerno. The captain said he would send the tags and the location to brigade HQ, with a request to send a patrol to extricate the bodies. It violated the warrior's code to abandon the dead, and although we'd had a good reason, it troubled me for a long time afterward.

Finding Barbara Lindstrom's phone number was easy enough. Not so easy was working up the nerve to call, tell her who I was, what I had seen four decades ago, and what we had failed to do. After I did, she was silent for so long that I thought we'd been disconnected.

"Mrs. Lindstrom?" I said.

"Barbara," she answered. "You can call me Barbara. I'd like to talk to you in person."

We met for lunch the next day at a diner in Riverside, which isn't all that far from my place in San Diego. Barbara was an ample woman whose graying black hair, cut short and tightly curled, called to mind an Astrakhan cap. For all her professions of chronic sorrow, she was rather cheerful and open, telling me that her brother had been a patriot; he'd dropped out of his first year of college to join the army because he wanted to carry on in the tradition of his father and uncles, who had fought against evil in Europe and the South Pacific. That was how he saw things then, she said. The war was a war of good against evil. And how proud the family had been when he won a Bronze Star for heroism!

Had I known Paul? I shook my head, then showed her my notebook and went through my story again, editing out the graphic details. (Salerno, I'd remembered, had been the one missing a good part of his face and head). She opened a small album containing two newspaper clippings from the *Bergen County Register*, one recounting the actions for which her brother had been awarded the decoration, the other, dated several weeks later, announcing that he was missing and presumed dead.

"Oh, I will never forget the day that car parked in front of our house and an army chaplain and an officer got out. It was a Saturday, I wasn't in school, and my mom and dad knew why those men were there. My mother collapsed, my father answered the door, and. . ."

She shut her eyes and pressed the back of her head against the booth. I wondered if I ought never to have contacted her; it seemed all I'd done was to refresh her grief. But she composed herself and turned a page in the album to show me an eight-by-ten photograph of Paul in uniform. I looked at it for hardly more than a few seconds, distracted by an object she pulled from a pocket in the album's cover—the dog tags that I hadn't seen in four decades. They had been sent to his family with his medals and personal effects.

"But it's him I want," she said. Thirty years in California had not ironed the Jersey out of her accent. "Don't care if it's a rib, a finger. Something, *anything*, I can put in the ground and say, 'There's my brother, Paul Salerno.'"

"Closure," I said.

She winced. "I can't stand that word. There's no closure. Not ever. I just want to bring him home. God knows, I sure tried to find out what had happened to him, where he might be. But got nowhere. Do you know why? Because there was no record of exactly where Paul had been killed."

"That's weird. I remember turning in these map coordinates. Maybe they got lost?"

She shrugged. "I wrote letters and emails to the Defense Department, to our congressman, our senator. Never got anywhere. The best thing about banging your head against a stone wall is that it feels great when you stop. So, I stopped. But you . . . it seems you're the only one with an idea of where he might be. Is there anything you can do?"

I answered that I didn't know, but would try. I picked up the check. Barbara borrowed the waitress's pen and wrote on a napkin and passed it to me.

"That's the department that accounts for MIAs," she said, "Paul isn't really an MIA, he's listed as"—she made air quotes—"'Killed in Action, Body Not Recovered.' You should start with them."

After I returned home, I emailed the department (it was called JPAC, for Joint POW/MIA Accounting Command) describing what we'd seen that day in 1969, what we'd done. I mentioned the *60 Minutes* segment that had led me to Barbara Lindstrom. Eventually, an army colonel replied, a lieutenant colonel, actually. He told me that her efforts had, in fact, inspired an attempt to find Salerno's remains a few years ago. It had failed to turn up a thing; however, since I'd been an eyewitness—and eyewitnesses were rare—he would try to persuade the Command to mount another attempt. Two weeks, maybe three, passed before I heard from him—approval had been granted. The fact that Paul Salerno's case had been aired on the oldest, most successful news broadcast in TV history probably had a lot to do with the decision.

Obtaining the required visas and permits, from our government as well as from the authorities in Hanoi, consumed a few more weeks. The colonel phoned me with the news. Although he was eager for me to, in his words, "join the team," he tried to talk me out of it. Rugged work. Could take a long time to find anything. Or to prove definitively that there was nothing to be found. Surely I remembered the climate—triple digit temperatures, humidity to match. Might be too much on a sixty-two-year-old man. I counterpunched: I'd been a gym rat for years and was in good shape, *damned* good shape, for someone my age. I would not be a hindrance. He threw out another objection: the Command was reluctant to send people who had an emotional stake in the outcome of a search—relatives of the MIA, old war buddies . . . I stopped him right there.

"I never knew those guys. No emotions involved. I just feel a sense of responsibility."

What turned his qualified yes into a definite yes was the fact that I'd been a medic in the army and a medical technician afterward. I might be of use to the recovery team's doctor.

I kissed Delia goodbye (she thought I'd gone a bit off my rocker; so did my three daughters and everyone else in the family except my eldest son-in-law, Jared. He said it would be a mitzvah, *a super* mitzvah. I thought of it more as an atonement). I flew to Command headquarters at Hickam Field in Hawaii, where I met up with the team: an archeologist; a forensic anthropologist; a doctor, and a detachment of American soldiers commanded by a captain who specialized in recovering the missing. We lingered at Hickam for a couple days. I should say that *I* lingered, idle while the others organized equipment, attended briefings, finalized travel arrangements.

On our last afternoon there, the captain, name of Byers, met me at the base swimming pool. Over gin and tonics, he began to grill me about what I'd seen on that day, April 4, 1969. What kind of uniforms were the KIA's wearing? Mottled camouflage or tiger stripe? Any name tags on their shirts? He went on, asking for details I didn't know or had forgotten; and though I was happy to provide what little intelligence I had, I grew impatient.

"Captain, I've already gone over everything I can remember. What's with all these questions?"

My tone ruffled him a bit. He wasn't the sort of man you wanted to ruffle—a veteran of Iraq, six-two or -three, an intimidating presence.

"Because I'm trying to make a tough job a little easier. Do you know why the last recovery mission came out a bust?"

"Salerno's sister told me that there were no records of when and where her brother disappeared."

"There aren't, but after we got your information, I researched this case, through channels and outside of them. I found a post-flight report from the pilot who evacuated the KIAs. There wasn't a lot in it, but his coordinates jibe with yours, and the date. Otherwise, there's zero. Zilch."

I looked at him, shrugging and spreading my hands to ask what this meant.

"The hardest recoveries are the ones that involve MIAs who were on black ops missions," he answered. "There's no documentation because those missions were highly classified."

'You're saying that. . ."

"I'm ninety percent sure, yeah. Officially, on paper, whatever unit those five troopers belonged to didn't exist. So, in a way, neither did they."

"So how do your questions make things any easier?"

"Every little scrap of information helps. And right now, you're the man with the scraps."

Early the following morning, we boarded a commercial flight, crossed the Pacific and the East China Sea, landed in Hanoi, and flew on to Danang. A day later, jet-lagged to the marrow, I found myself on the hill where I had last seen the corpses of PFC Chandler and Corporal Salerno.

I knew it was the right hill only because the GPS coordinates matched those in my notebook. Otherwise, I recognized almost nothing. The jungle was no longer a jungle; most of the towering teak and mahogany trees had been felled by loggers. The banyan had likewise been cut down. In the village in the valley below (where the team pitched its base camp), the thatch and bamboo huts of the past had been replaced by brick and stucco-faced bungalows; the buffalo cart trail that once led to it, across rice paddies and sugar-cane fields, had been widened into a laterite road to accommodate the logging trucks; and where kerosene lamps once flickered, electric lights now burned. The only thing familiar, aside from the stifling heat, was the landscape to the west—the Truong Son Mountains, immense green waves in arrested motion, heaving and falling and bluing with distance, vanishing at last into a lilac haze at the horizon.

Byers and his co-team leader, Martha Prine—the anthropologist, a tanned, rangy woman with squint lines at the corners of her gray eyes—were upset; they hadn't been told about the logging operation. Whatever remains had survived four decades in the ground might not have survived cutting crews stomping around, machinery dragging fallen timber.

Every morning, we convoyed from base camp to the hill, then hiked a footpath to the top, lugging high-tech stuff like gyrotheodolites and communications gear and laser range finders, and low-tech stuff like picks and shovels. Villagers were hired to build a bamboo frame for a screening station, and to wield the picks and shovels and post-hole augurs. Altogether, some forty people were employed in a hunt for the artifacts of a war that must have seemed, to everyone but me, as remote in time as Waterloo. The anthropologist, the archeologist, the soldiers, the villagers hacking holes into the hilltop—all were under forty. Only the interpreter, Nguyen Trinh, had memories of the war, and his were childhood memories.

The soil was clay, a yellow clay with the consistency of not-quite hardened cement. Its resistance seemed almost intentional, as if it were determined to keep its secrets. I pitched in where I could, laying transit tape, digging here, digging there, helping out at the screening station where water was sluiced through dirt, ferried from the excavation sites by a bucket line of villagers; then the mud was sifted for anything that looked human or man-made. Vietnam's soil is acidic: it eats away at bones, cloth, at almost any material this side of plastic. A week's work, in air that felt like a warm mask clamped over our faces, produced a Kevlar helmet, a shredded poncho, and what appeared to be part of a femur. There was no name tape in the helmet, which wasn't a relevant find anyway—the dead soldiers hadn't been wearing helmets. As for the femur, Prine identified it as a monkey's.

I struck up a friendship with Trinh, a stocky, broad-faced man who wore a faint mustache that lent him a slightly unsavory look. He spoke nearly flawless English, and for some reason took a liking to me. At the end of one particularly hard day, he mentioned to Prine and me that some three hundred thousand North Vietnamese soldiers were missing and unaccounted for, compared with less than two thousand Americans. He made that observation apropos of nothing, and did not elaborate, but left us with the clear impression that he regarded all the effort and expense to recover and repatriate our own dead as an indulgence, something like the huge PXs we'd built during the war, overflowing with luxuries his people couldn't imagine. Maybe that was so. Prine, who'd worked with Trinh on a previous expedition, took the view that we were engaged in a "sacred task." And maybe that was so as well. I remembered Barbara Lindstrom's words: "Something, *anything*, I can put in the ground and say, 'There's my brother, there's Paul.'"

Midway through the second week, with no results, I began to doubt myself. I had raised Barbara's hopes; she would be crushed if we came up empty-handed. Prine counseled patience. The bodies may have been buried nearby, by whom, she couldn't say. The villagers? I asked. No, said Trinh; he'd spoken with the elders, and no one could recall any burial parties. *Please*, Prine implored. It's only been ten days. The coordinates match. We're where we should be. Something usually remains, despite the corrosive soil. Give it time. She had taken part in one search on a South Pacific island that lasted a *year*, but eventually unearthed the partial skeleton of a marine missing in action since 1944.

Later on, Trinh offered a different kind of encouragement after I told him about Barbara's recurrent dream and how I'd been struck by its similarity to what I'd seen. A coincidence? Trinh lit a cigarette—he was seldom without one—and stared at me through a veil of smoke.

"Yes, that is a possibility, but not the only one."

While interviewing the locals, he'd heard from an elder that two ghosts had haunted the village and its environs in the past. People had seen them in the night mists, had heard their dire moans on the night winds. "I think they were the ghosts of the men we are looking for," Trinh said, quite matter-of-factly. They had become "wandering souls," *cò hõn,* caught in a limbo between this world and the next, unable to find rest because they had died violently and had not been properly buried in their native ground.

The war had overpopulated the country with these itinerant spirits. Trinh's uncle, a political commissar during the war, had been one. He'd gone missing on the Ho Chi Minh Trail, probably vaporized in a B-52 bombing raid. For a long time afterward, he visited Trinh's aunt in dreams, crying out to her, startling her awake. She consulted a holy man noted for his wisdom, and he advised her to build a tomb for her husband and to leave food offerings there at the Festival of Wandering Souls, *Têt Trung Nguyen*. Her husband's spirit would then have a home and cease to haunt her. This she did, and the dreams troubled her no more.

We happened to be in the Month of Wandering Souls, the seventh on the lunar calendar, when the trees drip tears and the moon weeps. Tomorrow, the 15th, said Trinh, would be the day set aside for the festival. Ceremonies would be held in the village. Perhaps you would like to observe them? he asked, and I answered that perhaps I would.

In the morning, the sun a crimson eye glaring down on the world, he and I joined a pilgrimage to the windy tombs in the village cemetery. They looked like miniature pagodas and were called windy because they were empty. Empty, that is, of corporeal remains. Rice cakes and lentil cookies were laid at the entrances to provide the deceased's' spirits with nourishment. Prayers were said. Then we filed down a paddy dike to the village temple, the women resembling mushrooms in motion under their conical straw hats. Leaving our shoes and sandals outside, we went in and sat cross-legged on reed mats before a lacquered altar decorated with strings of lights like Christmas tree lights. Photographs of the dead were propped against the altar, on which joss sticks smoked in glass vases. An ordained monk in a saffron robe and two novitiates in red sat facing us, their shaved, bronze heads reflecting the lights.

The monk, hands folded in his lap, began a chant. He sat perfectly still, only his lips moving. When he fell silent, the novitiates took it up.

Their call-and-response was repeated again and again, all in Pali, the ancient tongue, Sanskrit given voice. Of course, I didn't understand a word—neither did Trinh, for that matter—yet that drone, monotonous and hypnotic, seemed to pluck a chord inside me so that I grasped its meaning: it was a chant of lamentation and remembrance and appeal.

The temple was open on all sides, but no breeze blew. Lulled by the monks' prayers, I felt drowsy in the sultry air. My chin dropped to my chest, my eyes closed, and for an instant—no more than that—I saw them, imprisoned in the banyan roots. It was a kind of flashback, a re-creation if you will, but with one exception: Chandler and Salerno were alive, clutching the twisted roots, mouths agape in a silent shout—or a scream. This dream or vision, as vivid and startling as it was brief, jolted me awake. It lingered in my mind for a few moments, as an after-image does on the retina, and fear lingered with it. But when the ritual ended and we all shuffled out of the temple, I said nothing to Trinh.

That night, in the tent the doctor and I shared, I cut an Ambien in half with a razor—Ambien was my jet-lag cure—shook out a malaria pill from its bottle, and washed both down with warm canteen water, bitter with the taste of purification tablets.

"You really shouldn't mix them," the doctor cautioned. I haven't introduced him. His name was Mark Lujan, a New Mexican who claimed direct descent from a Spanish settler who had been among the founders of Santa Fe. It was hard for an old man like me to accept him as a major and a fully-fledged MD; he couldn't have been more than thirty, a redhead whose freckled face made him look younger still.

"Lariam can have some weird side-effects, so does Ambien," he said. "The two together? Not a great cocktail."

I lay down on my cot and secured the mosquito net's Velcro straps to the cot's poles. "I read the warnings. No problems so far."

"Malarone is just as effective against malaria, and no side effects. You have to take it every day instead of once a week, that's the only drawback. I can start you on it after the Lariam wears off."

"You're the doctor."

The camp's generator thumped outside. A small, oscillating fan, pedestaled on a storage box, swept back and forth. I bundled my clothes under my pillow to make a neck rest, strapped on a headlamp, and opened a paperback, a Michael Connelly mystery. I'd read only a couple of pages before my eyes grew heavy. I turned the headlamp off and fell asleep in seconds.

I didn't need the headlamp to find my way to the latrine; a full moon turned the post-midnight blackness into twilight. My shadow as I walked was distinct on the whitened ground, a cutout of myself. I saw them when I turned to start back to the tent: apparitions that cast no shadows but were shadows themselves, upright, definitely human in form but without faces or hair or features of any kind, just two grayish silhouettes blocking my path. Feeling vulnerable and exposed in my near nakedness—I was wearing only boxer shorts and flip-flops—a cry rose in my throat and died there. Sweat shellacked me scalp to toes, and it wasn't due to the muggy air. The specters began to move away, drifting like fog yet retaining their human shape. Each raised an arm, beckoning me to follow, and I did, in spite of my terror. I could not feel the ground beneath my feet, could see nothing but Chandler and Salerno, or, rather, their spirits. It was as if we three were floating through a void. They stopped, and right then pointed toward the mountains, and I understood what they were trying to tell me.

Someone grabbed my arm and shook me and called me by name, called right into my ear. It was the doctor. His freckles were plain to see in the moonlight.

"Hey! Hey!" he said. "Are you awake? Are you all right?"

Confused, disoriented, I didn't answer. Looking around, I saw that I was outside the camp, on the road that led toward the search site.

"What the hell. . . ?" I started to ask.

"Walking in your sleep."

He'd gotten up to go to the latrine shortly after I had, and had seen someone on the road. Thinking nothing of it at first, he returned to our tent, noticed that my cot was empty, and realizing that I was the figure on the road, came after me.

"Your eyes were open and glassy and blank. Classic sleepwalker. Lay off the Ambien. Sleepwalking is one of the side effects."

We started back. The shadows of the trees, flung across the road, looked like fallen logs missing one dimension.

"I had a weird experience," I said in an undertone. "Two weird experiences. Like dreams but I'm not sure they were dreams."

I told him about the Wandering Souls and described the brief vision in the temple and the one I'd had minutes ago. "It was so damned *real.* Not like most dreams, all jumbled up. It was clear as could be. They told me that they're buried somewhere in the mountains. I don't mean they spoke, it was kind of like mental telepathy."

Lujan mused for a while and gave his diagnosis when we were again inside the tent: Lariam sometimes produced vivid, disturbing, narrative dreams that were, for all practical purposes, hallucinations. He cupped my knee in his hand. "That spooky ceremony you went to, the stories about hauntings and wandering ghosts—the power of suggestion. Stir that in with your pharmaceutical cocktail, and it's not surprising you saw things that aren't there." He stretched his lips into a wide grin, and when he did, he reminded me of the red-haired character in MAD Magazine, What-Me-Worry. He was too young, I suppose, to remember MAD Magazine. "This will stay between us," he said. "Martha, y'know, was kind of leery about you working with us. That you might have flashbacks or something."

"You can tell Miz Prine, no worries about me freaking out, okay?"

"I'm not going to tell her anything."

The doctor's analysis of my strange visions was reasonable, rational, medically sound; but sometimes rationalism is overrated.

By the beginning of the third week, the hilltop looked like a gigantic tic-tac-toe board: plastic tapes staked out search sections ten feet square, each pitted with holes or shallow trenches that could, with a little imagination, be taken for Xs and Os. I again pitched in at the screening station and was shaking the screen, like an old-time placer miner, when Dexter—the archaeologist who was in charge of the station—yelled "Stop!" He plucked a tiny, aquamarine object from the dirt, which I thought was a gemstone of some kind. "It's a tooth!" he cried out. "We found a tooth!" The news traveled along the bucket line to the teams excavating the hilltop, and Byers and Prine came running. A moment later, Dexter spotted another, tinted the same dull, bluish-green as the first.

Prine wiped her forehead with her sleeve and gaped at the teeth as if they were gold nuggets.

"Wonderful, oh, this is wonderful," she said.

"Two teeth?" I said. I'd hoped for something more substantial.

"Yes! Teeth are much more resistant to the acids in this soil than bone, and we can compare them with dental records." With the care of an evidence tech at a crime scene, she plucked the teeth from the clay clods with tweezers and placed them in a plastic bag. "Look like molars, and one has a filling. Everyone is gaga these days about DNA, but teeth . . . they're just as good. Maybe better."

The mood at lunch was celebratory. The villagers shared in the excitement—frankly, I didn't know why—and cooked up a feast of *pho* and sticky rice with chicken. Prine hoisted a glass of beer and said, "Here's to the tooth fairy," and we echoed her, "The tooth fairy!" and laughed. Soon after, Dexter and his crew headed back to the site. Prine and Byers stayed in the mess tent with Lujan, Trinh, and me—I was worn out, not quite the sixty-plus stud I'd made myself out to be. The captain and Prine were discussing how to proceed next when someone outside summoned Trinh from the table. Twenty minutes later, as we were about to leave, our linguist reappeared, accompanied by a peculiar figure: an old man armed with a crossbow and arrows in a hollow bamboo tube belted to his waist. A cork pith helmet covered his head, sandals cut from used car tires were on his gnarly feet, and some sort of robe was rolled up and thrown sash-like across his chest. His face—round, pale brown, deeply seamed—reminded me of a worn catcher's mitt. He squatted down outside, resting the crossbow on his knees.

The man's name was Lham and he was a Montagnard—a hill tribesman—who lived in a distant village in the mountains. He'd heard about us and what we were looking for, Trinh explained, without informing us how this communication had been effected in a place without telephones, much less internet connections. Because the Montagnard spoke halting Vietnamese, and he, Trinh, barely a word of Lham's tribal language, he couldn't be sure he'd completely understood what the man had said; but he'd understood enough and knew we needed to hear it.

Trinh sat down, put on a grave expression, and lit the inevitable cigarette. "The bodies not here. They are buried in this man's village. It is maybe two days from here by walking."

I did not react outwardly, you know, drop my spoon into my bowl of pho in amazement; but I did turn my gaze to the doctor, who squinted back at me with a look I couldn't interpret.

"How did they get there, the bodies?" asked Prine, looking at Trinh skeptically.

"Him and his friends brought them there."

"They carried the bodies for two days? Through the mountains? When?"

"Many, many years ago, Miss Martha. The bodies not bodies, only bones."

"Skeletons?"

"I think so."

"And you believe him?"

"He is *moi*, you know," answered Trinh, using the Vietnamese pejorative for the Montagnards. It means "savages." "And the *moi*, it is hard to know when they are telling the truth. But, yes, I think I believe him."

Not long after the war, Trinh narrated, in 1977 or 1978 as best as he could figure, Lham and a few companions had been hunting for meat. They'd wandered to this place, far from their home grounds because the war had made game scarce. Lham shot a monkey out of a tree with his crossbow. When he bent down to pick up the animal, he saw, behind the tree's hanging roots, two human skeletons, shreds of uniform hanging from their ribs.

"It was as you described it," Trinh added, looking at me. "A banyan tree."

He continued: A couple of Lham's friends had fought as irregulars with the American Special Forces. They knew by the size of the skeletons that they had discovered what was left of two American soldiers. The hunting party decided among themselves to bury them on the spot. Not doing so would bring very bad luck from the dead men's spirits. They chopped at the roots with their machetes, opening a hole through which they were able to drag the skeletons out. Their plan had been to dig graves with the machetes and their bare hands, but both blades and hands barely scratched the hard clay. They debated what to do, deciding finally to send one man back to their village for proper tools. While he was gone, Lham and the others camped out, subsisting on monkey meat. The man returned empty-handed days later. He'd been told to bring the bones to the village and bury them there. And that is what they did.

No one said anything. I sat in wonderment, sweat dripping off my nose into my soup bowl. Another coincidence? That's what the doctor would call it (what he did, in fact, call it that night, before we went to sleep). My Lariam-induced dream had been proven true in an astounding coincidence. But I knew that something extraordinary had happened to me a few nights earlier, so I gravitated to Trinh's viewpoint: coincidence was a possibility, yes, but not the only one.

Poor Chandler and Salerno, decaying in their root-barred coffin for years! I glanced at Lham, squatting in the dirt, his expression impassive. Shame flashed through me, picturing him and his fellow tribesmen trudging through the bush with their burden of rattling bones. They might have interred them out of self-interest—bad things would befall them if they didn't—yet they had done what I and Sergeant Sanchez had failed to do.

Byers—he was sitting next to me—switched on his laptop, opened a topo map of the surrounding area, and asked Trinh if he could pinpoint Lham's village. Prine raised a hand, palm facing out.

"Let's not start planning expeditions just yet," she said, then turned to Trinh. "Please ask Mr. Lham if he's absolutely positive they were Americans and if he can show us where they're buried."

Trinh relayed her questions, which Lham answered in the affirmative. He then said something more, provoking from Trinh a single, high-pitched word that struck our ears as a squeal. The two fell into an exchange that went on for several minutes, the expression on Trinh's face shifting from surprise to a scowl to bewilderment. The old man's face retained its unreadable serenity, his responses models of monosyllabic economy, probably because he wasn't fluent in Vietnamese, though it appeared he could understand it well enough. At one point, Prine tried to interrupt, but Trinh silenced her with a brusque wave. He sounded angry with Lham, but it was hard to tell. Vietnamese is a tonal language, and its sharps and flats, its quick rises and falls, can make even a mundane conversation sound like an argument.

Finished, Trinh fished another smoke from the pack in his shirt pocket.

"What was that all about?" Prine asked in a surly voice. She hadn't liked the dismissive way he'd silenced her. "Clue us in."

"He says that his friends and him buried the bones and that the American who was living in their village piled rocks on their grave to mark them. Many rocks, like shrine. Lham knows where it is. He can show us."

"An *American*? What American?"

"The one in their village. He was the one who told the men to bury bones in the village cemetery. He is now there."

Trinh spoke in a distant voice, as if he did not quite believe his own words.

"So . . . you mean to tell us . . . this old man means to tell us, there are *three* Americans buried there?"

"Oh, no, Miss Martha. This American is still alive."

Lham's account shocked us into a state, equal parts astonishment and curiosity, leavened with disbelief. Who hadn't heard misty rumors about gray-haired ex-GIs glimpsed in isolated jungle hamlets? Prine scorned. Alluring myths that belonged in the same category as Bigfoot sightings.

"A few years ago, the media jumped all over a story about a POW way up in the hills in the North," she said. "A total hoax. The guy was part French, part Vietnamese, but he looked more white than Asian and thought he could make a few bucks passing himself off as an American."

And Lham's tale? A Bigfoot sighting?

She sat the old man down and questioned him, a frustrating exercise owing to the difficulties in negotiating three languages. What is the American's name? Lham's answer sounded like "Eejon." Prine's forehead crinkled. Trinh asked him again, and this time he replied, "Ongjon." "He means *Ông John*," said Trinh. "Mister John." That was all? Mister John? Yes. What does he look like? Like an American. How old is he? He is old now. How long has he been living in your village? Long time. Had Mister John been an American soldier? Yes. Does he know we are here and why? Trinh appeared to have a hard time getting this last inquiry across; he and Lham jabbered back and forth for a while, an effort that yielded another terse reply: *Tôi không biết*—I don't know.

Prine threw Trinh a quizzical squint. There was more fractured conversation between him and the old man.

"He doesn't know if Mister John knows because Mister John is sick," Trinh translated. "He says he came here because he heard there is a doctor with us. He hopes the doctor can make Mister John better. The healer in the village could not."

That a man who may have been pushing seventy-five would trek through the bush for two days, merely on a rumor of medical help, spoke of a fierce loyalty, and more—devotion.

Prine started to interrogate Lham further, then seemed to think better of it. She leaned back in her camp chair, swiping a mustache of sweat from her upper lip while her eyes roamed over our faces. It was obvious from her pained expression that she was torn between the desire to find out if this tantalizing marvel were true and the reluctance to go off on what might prove to be a Bigfoot hunt. As for me, I reminded myself that my responsibility was to Barbara Lindstrom; her brother's remains were what I was after.

"So do we believe him?" Prine said to no one in particular. "It's all too fantastic."

"He was pretty specific," I said. "The banyan, the skeletons, the American's name—he can't be making it up. Why would he?"

"We don't have any choice, we've got to try," said Byers, sounding as if he were giving an order. "If we've got two of our own buried out there and, Christ, maybe another one still breathing, *we have got to try*."

"I'm aware of that," she snapped. "Finding whatever's left of the two MIAs—no problem if Lham really can take us to them. Our big problem is this guy, this Mister John. Who the hell is he? Is he really an American? What's he doing there and what do we do about him? How can we pack up this whole operation and move it thirty, forty miles through the bush *on foot*? We'll need to be flown in. That means helicopters. And that means we'll have to contact our military attaché, and he'll have to get authorization from their Ministry of Defense. If it leaks that maybe, just maybe, we've got a live American out there. . ."

She sighed, leaving the rest unsaid.

Byers scooped up some now-cold sticky rice with his chopsticks, then twirled them to indicate that he was mulling things over. "All right. How about a recon? A stripped-down crew, carrying essential supplies and gear. You, me, a couple of my troops, the doctor. We'll need him if this Mister John is sick. We stay in radio contact with base camp. We get a picture of the situation, take it from there. Assess, adapt, improvise. The army way."

"Sounds a bit too improvisational," Prine said. "Sounds pretty damn close to rogue."

"Rogue? Hell, no."

"Standard procedure would be that we contact the attaché," she said.

"This isn't what I'd call a standard situation. We've gotten intel, most of it sketchy. We need to check it out before committing resources. Nothing rogue about that."

"Dexter and the others. . . ?"

"We tell them we're checking out a report that the remains might be in another location. Nothing about this Mister John. Too much risk of a leak. If the time comes for them to know, we let them know."

I'm not sure I like that," she said, without enough confidence to overcome Byers's. "Let's think it through before we take another step."

"If you decide to take it, I'm going," I said.

Prine and the captain shook their heads almost in unison.

"It would be essential personnel only," he said.

"I'm not asking permission. None of you would be here if it wasn't for me. I'd say that makes me damn essential."

I am normally not so pushy, but I felt under an obligation. I refrained, of course, from mentioning that Salerno's ghost—his spiritual remains, so to speak—had directed me where to find his mortal remains.

Lujan stepped in. "I'd like to have him along. If the American, the maybe American, is sick, I might need some help."

The trek under a rainforest canopy that dimmed noon to dusk and darkened midnight into a blackness no eye could penetrate was a journey back in time, to my year in the war, and then further back, much, much further, to an epoch when plants and reptiles were sovereigns of the Earth. Trees, millions of trees over two hundred feet high, with buttress roots like sloping walls. The winners in the perpetual struggle to reach the light, the losers exterminated so that the avenues between those giants were free of saplings and wider than sidewalks, though matted with huge ferns that denied easy passage. Led by Lham, we followed a well-used trail through a river valley which showed on Byers's map as a white corridor hemmed by green, the green striated with crowded contour lines that indicated the steepness of the mountain slopes.

We had covered about five miles when we halted for a break, and became spectators to a fight between a small snake and a gargantuan centipede. The centipede was eight or nine inches long and, making no timid attempt to blend into its surroundings, flaunted vivid bands of red, yellow, and blue—colors that communicated a warning: Stay Away from Me! The snake ignored it and wrapped itself around the centipede, trying to sink its fangs into the insect. But the centipede clutched the serpent's body with its hundred legs, and the two, each holding the other in a repulsive embrace, writhed in the mud for a few minutes, the snake losing strength until the centipede killed it with a quick, venomous strike to its neck.

"I guess the lesson is, don't bring fangs to a leg fight," Byers quipped.

The jungle. The war between armed Homo sapiens had ended long ago, but that didn't mean the jungle was at peace; the Darwinian contest went on unabated, as it had for a hundred thousand years.

We were seven altogether, not including Lham: Prine, Lujan, Byers, Trinh, and me; Rojas, the radio operator; and Tonelli, skilled in the sort of excavations we would be doing; that is, grave-digging. "Like poking around in an ancient royal tomb," he'd told me. Each of us carried anywhere from twenty-five to fifty pounds. The radioman—"comm specialist," in Byers's parlance—had the heaviest burden, a high-tech marvel that made the radios we carried during the war seem as outdated as the telegraph. The rest of us packed a change of clothes and a supply of MREs, collapsible solar panels to power Lujan's and Byers's laptops, and sturdy paper bags for collecting bone fragments (paper because plastic collected moisture that could contaminate DNA). Lujan carried a kit containing remedies for every tropical disease in the diagnostic manual. I had bragged how fit I was, now I had to prove it, and proving it wasn't easy. I had some trouble keeping up. The air was so still and thick as to seem solid; a solid weight pressing down, pressing in from all sides. Byers, who marched right behind Lham, paused every now and then to keep track of our direction and the distance we'd traveled with his GPS. But that intricate thatch-work high overhead, blocking and diverting the satellite signals upon which the GPS relied, made it a less-than-trustworthy instrument. We had to put our faith in Lham and in old tech—the compass.

"This bring back old memories?" the doctor asked me during one of the captain's navigational checks.

I nodded. The most vivid memory was of the smell peculiar to the jungle, fetid and fragrant, the scents of decay and birth fused into a single odor; and that rank perfume and the vagrant sunlight retrieved a memory of fear. Not fear of getting shot or captured or bitten by a viper, but of becoming lost in that dripping green wilderness. Utterly, hopelessly lost.

We strung hammocks and lay down, lullabied by screeching monkeys and cicadas, and were on the move the next morning, when it was barely light enough to see more than five feet in front of your own face. The early start was necessary to cover ground before the mercury bumped the top of the thermometer. The valley floor rose gradually, narrowing as it rose, and the river narrowed with it to the breadth of a trout stream. What with the stale air and steep slopes close on either side and the webbed branches above and the dark water flowing past, we felt as though we were in an immense sewer. Byers consulted Lham about how much farther we had to go. His minimally informative response, "Not far," annoyed the captain. Trinh grew suspicious. Like all Vietnamese, he held Montagnards in low esteem. "Maybe he lie to us," he whispered to me, though he couldn't say why Lham would.

Around midday, we came to a waterfall, a paradisal spot where wild orchids ornamented the trees and the pool beneath the falls was deep and clear. We dropped our packs and jumped in, clothes and all, washing off the sweat and insect repellant varnishing our skin. The Montagnard sat on a rock, the crossbow in his lap, and watched us, splashing each other like children. After the restorative dip, we climbed to the top of the falls and walked out of the jungle onto a broad plateau stretching away to a range of purplish hills. It was a relief to be out of the claustral forests, to see the sky again in its entirety rather than as blue-white specks in the jungle's roof. A short distance off, dry rice fields terraced knolls ringing thatched roof longhouses that looked like huge, brown lozenges. Lham's village.

Byers radioed our arrival to base camp; then we followed our guide down a meandering footpath that widened into a dusty street, longhouses raised on stout, six-foot pilings on both sides. Wide decks made of lashed bamboo trunks extended from the open fronts, with notched logs propped against them as ladders. Women weaving on looms, old men smoking cheroots, kids in motley getups pieced together from aid agency donations looked with wary curiosity at the strangers who'd intruded on their isolated world.

Lham brought us to a house at the edge of the village. We climbed the log ladder into the dark, windowless interior. Two kerosene lamps hanging from the rafters were lit, revealing an interior furnished with reed-mat beds and nothing else. The town guest house, I supposed. My back ached, icepicks jabbed my shoulders. I shed my pack and flopped onto a bed, any excitement I might have felt dampened by exhaustion. Byers, who could now take accurate readings with the GPS, announced that we had covered thirty-three miles, and were within a kilometer of the Laotian border.

Lham, who looked no more affected by the long march than I would be by a stroll across the mall, left us, returning about half an hour later with the village chief, Glun, a man of forty-five or fifty wearing a sun helmet and a San Antonio Spurs T-shirt. Trinh summoned Byers and Prine outside for a conference with this official, who, I gathered, spoke much better Vietnamese than Lham. Almost all the talking was between him and Trinh, occasionally interrupted by a question from Byers or Prine. The palaver went on for a while. When it was over, the captain called us together for a briefing. We sat in rough a semicircle around him, while the sun lowered toward the violet hills and people shambled in from the fields and the smell of wood cooking fires drifted in the listless air.

"So, here's the situation," Byers began. "They'll bring us to the gravesite tomorrow morning and we can get to work. But we're all thinking about the mystery man, right? Well, the chief wants the doctor to have a look at him, the doctor only. Not the way I want it, but nobody's had to deal with a thing like this before, so we'd best not push things too hard or too fast. This guy, if he really is a missing GI, he's like. . . Like those Japanese soldiers who turned up in the South Pacific thirty years after the war was over and didn't know it was over. And he's pretty sick. If all of us showed up at once, it might be too much on him." Byers ran his palms across the sweaty stubble at the sides of his head and looked at Lujan. "You're up to the plate. Do what you can for him. Find out whatever you can."

"A house call," Lujan said. He turned to Trinh. "Come with me, please, and ask the chief if I can bring my assistant."

He didn't need me, but I was pleased he'd made the request. We were going to set eyes on a myth made real—flesh, blood, and bone.

Mister John seemed to have attained an honored position among the Montagnards. His house, atop one of the low hills surrounding the village, shaded by a palm grove, with painted rocks bordering the path leading to its entrance, had a look of idyllic solitude. On the front deck, we were met by two people—an elderly woman in a brocade dress, like a sarong, and a man who might have been in his mid-thirties, tall, green-eyed, with a complexion two shades lighter than the woman's cherry-wood brown. He shook our hands and greeted us in English, which he must have learned from Mister John.

"Please meet you. Please come. Father sick."

He and the woman—presumably his mother—ushered us inside, dimly lit by a lamp flickering on a table beside a bamboo bed on which the object of our quest, the living object, that is, lay flat, dressed in a striped robe. It was knotted, toga-like, at the shoulder. Evidently, he'd been too ill to go outside to relieve himself; a slop bucket at the foot of the bed threw off an acrid stink. The young man leaned over him and spoke to him softly. He sat up slowly, grimacing as he did, and stared at us, his glassy eyes the same pale jade as his son's, his face yellowed by the lamplight, or, possibly, his disease. I'd expected a shaggy wreck, a half-starved Robinson Crusoe; but his hair and beard were neatly trimmed, and though he was thin, he did not look emaciated. A large, aquiline nose, bent slightly sideways at the tip, was his most distinctive feature, and it teased me with the eerie feeling that I'd seen him before.

"Mister John? Ông John?" said Lujan.

His head bobbed, he blinked. If he was amazed or shocked by our presence, he didn't show it. Lham or the chief must have prepared him for our arrival; on the other hand, he may have been too ill to display any emotion.

"I'm a doctor, Doctor Lujan. This man helps me out. We're going to try to make you better."

He didn't move or speak, just kept staring and blinking.

"You understand what I'm saying?"

Another curt nod. He worked his jaw back and forth, and we realized that he hadn't heard English for so long that he scarcely remembered how to speak it himself, aside from the few words of pidgin he probably exchanged with his son.

"Are you in any pain?"

"Ye-es."

"Where?"

With a quaking hand, he touched his shoulders and knees. "Here, too," he said, opening and closing his fist.

Dipping into his rucksack, Lujan withdrew a stethoscope, a thermometer, a blood pressure gauge, and a small notebook, which he handed to me, instructing that I record the patient's vitals. He loosened the knot of Mister John's gown, baring a chest reddened by a white-specked rash, and began the examination. Temperature—102.5. Blood pressure—99/62. Pulse—118. He put on surgical gloves, shined a pen light into the sick man's nostrils, which were clogged with hair, then parted his lips. His teeth bore dark red stains, like the kind that comes from betel nut, but were in fact dried blood. Blood oozing from his gums.

The doctor whispered, "He's missing two back teeth."

"Like the ones we found?"

"Maybe. Not sure," he said, then rolled down his shirt sleeves, spritzed his face and hands with Deet, and flipped the repellant to me. "He's got dengue. You don't want to get bit by a mosquito that's bitten him."

A mosquito was singing in my ear at that moment, and I had to fight an urge to run out of that dim, stifling, malodorous room.

Lujan returned to Mister John. "Have you been sick like this before? Fever? A rash? Pain in your joints?"

Mister John spread two fingers.

"*Twice* before?"

"Uh-huh."

"You've got dengue fever, and I'm afraid there's nothing I can do for it. There's no cure for it except to wait it out," said Lujan, reaching again into his rucksack for a packet of Tylenol and a plastic water bottle.

"Take two of these. It's for the pain."

Mister John followed doctor's orders. Turning to the four people sitting on the floor, watching us with the attentive silence of a courtroom jury, Lujan passed the pills and the water to Mister John's son.

"Trinh," he said. "Explain that he should give his father two tablets twice a day and to make sure he drinks plenty of water. And for Christ's sake, get somebody to empty that stinking honey bucket."

While that was being done, Lujan sat down beside his patient and, putting on his best bedside manner, said that we were very curious about him and had a few questions, if he felt well enough to answer. Otherwise, we would leave him alone for now.

To this, the sick man had no reaction whatsoever.

"Do you mind?"

"Go . . . 'head."

By way of preamble, enunciating slowly, as if speaking to a foreigner (which in a way Mister John was), the doctor spelled out that we belonged to a team that recovered the remains of GIs missing in action. We'd learned from Lham that two had been buried in this village at Mister John's direction, which was how we'd learned about him. We'd been searching for the missing soldiers east of here, where this man (motioning at me) had seen their bodies during the war, trapped in the roots of a tree. A banyan tree. This man was in the war. . . .

Now, Mister John did react; he made a jerky movement with one hand, his febrile eyes flicked to me, their expression focused, intense, and yet unreadable.

"You. . . . In it? . . . The war?"

I nodded. "A medic, yes."

"Were you a GI then?" Lujan pressed.

Mister John didn't answer, his gaze fixed on me.

"Mister John? Were you in the war?" the doctor repeated.

"Ye-es. Four. Spech all . . . Spech-a-list Fourth Class." He was beginning to get a firmer grip on his native language.

"Specialist Fourth Class what? Your name?"

He motioned at an object under his bed—a small sandalwood box. "Open."

Lujan did and pulled out a set of dog tags on a metal chain. He held them up to the light and said under his breath, "Well, holy shit, holy living shit," and passed the tags to me.

They read: Chriswell, John T., followed by a serial number.

"This is you? John Chriswell?"

He started to answer but then gulped and leaned over to retch into the bucket. He must not have eaten for quite a while; all that came out was the water he'd drunk, water tinged with greenish bile.

He wiped his lips with the back of his hand and said, "Sorry."

"Don't apologize. Vomiting—it's the dengue," said Lujan.

Once again, Mister John pinned his unsettling gaze on me. "You found bodies? Knew them? Sah . . . Salerno and . . . I forget other one."

"Chandler," I said, stunned. "How did you know who they were?"

"With them. Was with them. Escaped. Days in the bush, almost starved. Lham found me. Brought me here."

I said nothing until a number flashed in my memory. "Five. We had found five. You made it six? How, when. . . ?"

"Ye-es. Six," said Chriswell, formerly Mister John. He choked and vomited again, dry heaving this time.

"I think that's enough for now," Lujan said to me; then, to Chriswell: "Lie down. You need rest."

Dusk is brief in southern latitudes; daylight ditches to darkness in minutes. Byers and the others had vacated the longhouse. They were being fed and entertained in a large hut with a high, peaked roof and no walls. It was called a *Guol*, a kind of community center. Lanterns hung overhead, their light fogged by clouds of white moths. Women were cooking a rice and meat dish in bamboo tubes for their guests; a couple of men sat by a campfire outside, banging on brass gongs. We—Lujan, Trinh, and I—sat on a bench cobbled together out of logs and twine. As soon as we did, Prine and Byers half rose from their seats.

"Well?" Prine said. "Well?"

Lujan related some of what we'd learned, and I filled in the rest, recapping the saga Chriswell had condensed into a few broken sentences. Escaped. Days in the bush. Rescued and brought here.

A pretty girl offered me something to eat. I took the steaming bowl to be polite. The stench from the sick man's room clung to my nostrils, killing my appetite.

Byers booted up his laptop (amusing to see the message "No Internet") and clicked on the MIA database in its hard drive. He scrolled through the names, listed alphabetically, and soon hit: "Chriswell, John T. Spec. 4," and the notation, "MIA 4APR 69."

That drew another "holy living shit" from the doctor and a whistle from me.

"That confirms it," I said. "The same day we found Salerno and Chandler."

No one spoke for half a minute. The gong concert continued, and all the strangeness of our surroundings, the enigma Chriswell presented, seemed to be contained in that eerie, metallic percussion.

"I second your holy living shit," Byers said at last. "Missing since sixty-nine and we find him alive and well."

"Not so well," said Lujan.

"Right. But in a lot better shape than Salerno and Chandler."

"His blood pressure is on the low normal side, and the low part worries me." Our freckled, What-Me-Worry doctor treated us to a brief medical discourse. There were several varieties of the dengue virus—serotypes, he called them. Someone who'd been infected with one serotype in the past ran a high risk of developing serious complications if he became infected with another. Chriswell had had the disease *twice* before, so his risk was greater still. "I can keep him stabilized with acetaminophen and hydrating him. But if he gets any worse, he'll need to be hospitalized. Meaning a medevac."

Byers pressed his thumbs into his chin, a grave expression on his lined, sunburned face. "Medevac, medevac," he murmured. "That is gonna be tricky, lots of questions from lots of people, our people, their people, that we're not ready to answer. So do what you can for him."

The next morning, while Lujan checked in on his patient, Lham and Glun brought us to the village cemetery. It lay in the rainforest, where the spirits of the tribe's ancestors lived forever. Tall trees with smooth, gray trunks, like cement pillars, shrouded graves, some marked by wooden funeral statues, some by shrines that resembled miniature longhouses, walls and roofs decorated with colored symbols whose meaning was as unintelligible to us as the Masonic emblem would have been to a Montagnard.

Lham pointed at a rock pile near the cemetery's edge, a funeral statue atop it—the figure of a seated man, his arms resting on his knees, his face turned upward, into which its maker had carved a mournful, pensive expression.

"Americans buried there," said Trinh.

Glun said something to him, which Trinh translated: "When the sadness reaches the sky, freedom can be reached." He shrugged to tell us that he was as puzzled by this declaration as we.

"Just to make sure, we have the chief's permission to dig here?" asked Byers.

"Yes. He says best thing that they be buried with their ancestors."

Tools were laid out: short-handled picks; folding shovels, like army entrenching tools, but smaller; a portable sieve; trowels and brushes and the paper bags. Byers and I roped off the site with yellow tape so that it resembled a crime scene; then we removed the statue, which seemed a little sacrilegious, and dismantled the rock pile. Tonelli began to dig; Prine shook the spoil through the sieve. The excavation had to be carried out carefully, to avoid damaging any remains, or the chance of missing some small fragment. A long time passed before Tonelli's shovel made a clunking sound and he said, "Got something!"

On his knees, he resumed digging, now with a trowel. He brushed the dirt away and whooped. "Here they are!" I looked down at a pair of human skulls lying side by side, one somewhat intact, the other shattered, with a dime-size hole in the lower left jaw. Most of its teeth were gone or fragmented, and a second hole, twice the size of a fist, gaped where the right temple and right eye socket had been. You didn't have to be a forensic expert to determine that a bullet had pulverized the teeth, then punched out the man's brains as it exited; you only had to be an ex-combat medic who had seen enough entrance and exit wounds to know that he didn't care to see any more.

Except for these. They touched me with joy.

"It's Salerno!"

Byers cautioned me not to make assumptions. Positive ID would not be made until the skulls were analyzed at the lab in Hawaii.

Tonelli gloved his hands, brushed more dirt from the skulls, and set them down in a display that bore a likeness to a fossil exhibit in a museum. Another three-way translation took place: Lham to the village chief in the tribal tongue, the chief to Trinh in Vietnamese, Trinh to Byers and Prine in English, telling them that further excavations would be unnecessary; we had found all there was to find.

"Where's the rest of them?" asked the captain. "Lham told us they buried the skeletons."

"They try, but too far, too hard to carry all the bones. So they take the heads only."

The picture of Lham and his companions disassembling Salerno and Chandler enroute wasn't pretty, but its practicality made sense.

We had enough for identification purposes, Prine said. And considering the acidic nature of the soil at lower elevations, it was lucky that the skulls had been interred in the more alkaline earth of the mountains. She photographed them from various angles, then placed them in the paper bags, and those into canvas sacks, to which she affixed ID tags with the date and place where their contents had been discovered. I asked to carry the sacks back to the village. It was a good half-mile; the sun was at its peak ferocity. Byers looked at me.

"They don't weigh much, captain."

With an indifferent shrug, he gave his okay. I think he understood why it was something I needed to do.

"I'll go with you," said Prine. "It's a chain of custody issue."

She walked with long strides. I practically had to jog to keep up with her.

"What do you think of our mystery man?" she asked. "The real deal or an imposter?"

"His name matches, the date he was listed missing jibes. He knew Salerno and Chandler. It's incredible. Bigfoot lives."

She gave a scornful laugh. "Yeah. But y'know, something about this seems off to me."

"Is that why you're not excited?"

"Nope. I'm not excited because if he is genuine and word leaks out, the media will be on us like flies on honey. The media and crackpot conspiracy theorists who'll be convinced that he's really a POW and that a whole lot of GIs are still imprisoned over here."

There was a lot of messaging between Byers and Dexter at base camp when we reassembled in our longhouse: Salerno's and Chandler's remains recovered, packed for eventual transfer to the lab.

"Listen, Dexter, we might need . . . uh . . . someone medevacked. Over."

"Roger that. Who? What's wrong?"

"Dengue. I'll get back to you later. Over and out."

Just then, Lujan came in from a visit with his patient. Sitting down, he mopped his face with his shirttail and announced that he'd spoken to Chriswell about a medical evacuation, which Chriswell refused.

"His life is here, he says, and if it has to end, it ends here."

"He doesn't realize we're here to bring him home?" asked Byers.

"What did I just say?" The heat had made Lujan irritable. "The guy is in his sixties. He's got to know most likely there's no family left in the States to go back to. But here? Wife, son, grandchildren. This *is* home."

We were all seated on the deck, hoping to catch a breeze. Byers looked at the village, with its wattling roofs and basket-weave walls, at the pigs and chickens rooting or scratching in the dust.

"He thinks *this* is home?"

"You said he's like those Japanese in the Second World War. Me, I'd say he's like the people I heard about growing up in New Mexico, the ones in the old days. Captured by Comanches when they were kids and when they were given a chance to go back to civilization, they said, 'No, Thanks.' Chriswell's like that except he wasn't captured."

"No, he deserted," Byers said with contempt. "What sort of shape is he in?"

"About the same as yesterday," Lujan answered. "I took his blood pressure when he was lying down, then when he stood up. It showed a postural drop. Not a big one, but enough. His blood pressure is too low as it is."

"Which means. . . ?"

"A risk of Dengue Shock Syndrome. He goes into that, and he'll die here, all right, and pretty quick."

Sunset offered its benediction. We sauntered over to the communal house, the Guol, where women again cooked for us and we asked each other questions no one could answer. Had Chriswell deserted and why? If he was repatriated, how would he react to personal computers and the internet and tablets and smart phones? How had his existence here been kept hidden from the outside world for so long? Isolated though it was, the village wasn't on Mars. The kids in western hand-me-downs, the chief wearing a San Antonio Spurs T-shirt.

The gong players presented another concert, accompanied by a wind instrument, some sort of flute—two thin bamboo tubes sprouting like rabbit ears from a hollow gourd. As on the night before, the music was a monotonous succession of simple notes, the same notes over and over, and because my pledge to Barbara Lindstrom had been fulfilled, the incomprehensible noise awakened in me a desire to be out of that alien place and on my way home.

Just then, the radio beeped—a text from base camp. Byers read the message aloud: A medevac had been laid on for the next morning. A helicopter would fly the patient to Danang, where he would be put on a plane for Hanoi and the French hospital there.

"The chopper will drop us off at base camp, so we'd best start packing our bags," he said, and turned to Prine. "You and me, we're going to have to explain what we've been doing here, explain who Chriswell is and what we know about him."

"Fine with me," she said. "But I imagine the attaché will want to have a chat with him when he's better. And the Viets' TC2. It won't be fine with me if there's a leak to the press."

I asked what TC2 was.

"Second Department," replied Trinh. "Military intelligence."

"I'm sure the attaché is going to slap a media embargo once he knows," Byers said. "Anyway. Chriswell is going to be evacked whether he likes it or not." He sighed with relief. Responsibility for Chriswell would be out of our hands as of the next morning. "I'd better let him know what's up. Anyway, I want to see this guy. Rojas, come with me."

He and the radioman returned in ten minutes. The captain looked pale. His eyes rose to the lanterns, haloed by the pale-winged moths, then pivoted to me.

"He wants to talk to you."

"Me?"

"Yeah, you, and no one but. I told him what's going to happen and all he did was ask for you. Insisted. He said you would understand."

"Understand what?"

"Hell if I know."

Mister John's wife, his son, and what I assumed were his grandchildren were gathered outside his longhouse, keeping vigil. They acted as though they'd been expecting me; the woman in her red and black brocade gave me a short head bow, the son a handshake and an invitation to "please to go in and see father."

The interior greeted me with its noxious smell. Chriswell's chamber pot, the five-gallon bucket, had been refilled since its emptying the day before. Clad in the same filthy robe, he sat crosswise on his bed, thin legs dangling over the bamboo frame, his back against a wall. The light from the oil lamps tinted his face, already tanned from years in equatorial sunlight, to a reddish-brown. With its lacquer of feverish sweat and its fixed, somber expression, it made an unsettling impression, reminding me of the wooden idols in the village cemetery.

"Sit," he said, his hand flicking at a round chair that had been hacked out of a log; it was all one piece: back, seat, stool.

The son came in for the bucket, emptied it outside, and returned it to its place at the foot of the bed. I thanked him from the bottom of my heart, though the stench lingered in the motionless air.

"So, Chriswell. . ." I began.

"Ông John. Mister John, please."

"All right, I heard that you want to talk to me. Because I would understand. Understand what?"

"Know I'm dying, Gone by morning."

I had no reply to this prediction.

"You were in the war. And you . . . found Salerno and Chandler and need tell you . . . to tell you what happened to Salerno," he said, drawing the words out of himself, with a half or quarter beat between each one.

"I know what happened to him. He was killed in an ambush."

"Not that. Inside. Where the changes happen. Here . . . here." He touched his forehead, then his chest, wincing as he did. Even slight movements were painful for him. Dengue's nickname is breakbone fever.

"And Chandler?" I asked.

He snorted. "Chandler. . . . Fucking new guy. Not in country long enough to fall under Captain Wolfe's spell."

"Who?"

He was silent for a short time, immobile as the funeral statues he resembled. I looked back at him, fixated on his hawk's bill nose. I didn't know why it drew me in.

This Captain Wolfe, Mister John croaked in reply, had been given an independent command, free rein in a free-fire zone, and no colonel or general, no one at all to answer to so long as he got the job done, the job being to destroy guerrilla base camps and clear the valleys of the farmers and villagers who provided the enemy with food and intelligence.

"Out-guerrilla the guerrillas. . . . The mission."

"Black ops?" I asked.

"Don't know what color the ops were, but Wolfe's eyes . . . black. . . . Skin pale, like plaster. Lumps of coal in a plaster bust, eyes like that. . . . Salerno . . . okay in the beginning. Good Catholic boy, believed in his own decency. That's what . . . his trouble."

"Sorry, I'm not tracking."

Salerno's faith in his decency was a flaw, he continued (though not in those exact words). He could not imagine himself doing the wrong thing. When he joined Captain Wolfe's company, he conceived of himself as a righteous crusader enlisted in a righteous cause; and this self-image blinded him to his own darker instincts. He didn't know he had any.

"But Wolfe knew. Those eyes . . . didn't look at you . . . *into* you. Looked into all of us. Looked into Salerno . . . liked what he saw. Wolfe had a talent for that, y'know. Could see if you had it in you. Like a coach can see. . . . Know what I mean?"

"Like a coach can see if some kid has natural abilities that he can develop?"

"Ye-es."

"How do you know all this? You and Salerno were that close?"

He shook his head with quick, convulsive movements; I couldn't tell if he was denying that they'd been friends or dismissing the question as unimportant.

"All right. What did this Wolfe see?"

"Killers. Liked to quote Mao—the people are the sea the guerrilla swims in. To beat the guerrilla fish dry up the sea. . . . Getting rid of the people." Mister John not only had fully recaptured his English, his voice had grown firmer, the pauses between words less frequent. "We operated out of a Yard village like this . . . Wolfe's HQ in a longhouse like this. He made Mao speech to Salerno when he reported in. Same speech he gave everyone. 'Make these dinks more afraid of us than they are of the VC. Inflict terror. . . . Our mission. Is that clear?' And Salerno said it was, and all the time those bright black eyes drilling into him. He couldn't stand it, that examination, and he looked away at three Nungs sitting against a wall. You know about Nungs?"

I nodded.

"Those three . . . company scouts and kind of Wolfe's personal bodyguard. Wore necklaces, rawhide cords strung with . . . Salerno first thought they were some sort of dried, brown fruits. Next second, saw . . . he was mistaken. Couldn't take his eyes off them and Wolfe said it was Nung custom, and was Salerno shocked? Disgusted? He answered, 'No, sir.' Wolfe said, 'You're going to do well with us,' and meant it because he could read your soul, and what he read in Salerno's was that his answer had been honest. Salerno not shocked. Uh-uh. Nungs's souvenirs fascinated him. The fascination of abomination."

The fascination of abomination? Those words rattled around in my head. I'd never heard anyone use a phrase like that.

Mister John motioned at the water bottle under his bed. Lujan must have left it for him.

I handed it to him. He took a swig, swished the water in his mouth and spit into the bucket. The stream was tinged pink—his gums were bleeding again.

"Maybe we should start over," I said. "Forget Salerno. Tell me something about yourself, like how you managed to hide out here all these years. Maybe you could begin by telling me how you lost those teeth."

"Fell. Hit a rock. Knocked them loose. Pulled them out with my fingers."

"Where? Where and when did you pull them out?"

"Back there," he said, with a lazy wave of one thin hand. "What difference does it make, where, when?"

"Do you mean where the patrol was ambushed? Near the banyan?" If I could get nothing else out of this interview, I could determine if the teeth the team had discovered had been his.

But he did not answer.

"Salerno's soul . . . ruined. Wolfe ruined it," he said. "He ruined everyone. The devil's disciple."

Slumping against the wall, he muttered something to the effect that the jungled mountains were the devil's realm. Then jumbled phrases spilled from his lips, like pieces of a verbal puzzle I had to put together to make any sense of them. It went something like this: The canopy blinded men to the open sky, in whose bright clarity they might have beheld the beauty of God; and it was likewise impenetrable to God's holy word. Where the voice and face of God were absent, so was God's grace. The invitation was then open to His adversary to fill the void and cause men to lose their way. Why, if the devil was not the jungle's sovereign, were there so many serpents in it? Pythons. Kraits. Vipers.

I stared at him, dumbstruck by this bizarre sermon, then I said: "Could you be a little more . . . uh . . . specific?"

He grinned or grimaced—I couldn't tell which. "Specific? Sure. . . . Salerno's first operation with the Wolfpack—that was what we called ourselves—his squad set up on a riverbank. Fishermen bringing weapons, ammo to the Victor Charlies in their sampans, and the squad's mission was . . . ambush them when they were offloading. And they did. Killed everyone. Three kids on board. Killed them, too. And the squad found . . . fish! Fishermen . . . not smugglers, just fishermen! Salerno felt sick. Next day, in base camp, he didn't say one goddamn word to anybody. Know why?"

Mister John paused, apparently expecting me to reply, so I said that I had no idea why.

"Because he couldn't get what he'd seen out of his head. Wolfe pissed. Didn't want to think he'd been wrong about Salerno. Called him into his tent and told him, 'We're here to kill Communists and anyone who feeds Communists is a Communist and we kill them, too.' Those dinks . . . Fair game. And Salerno said that when he looked at those kids' . . . shredded little bodies, all he could think was 'God forgive me.' Wolfe came back. In the jungle . . . kill or be killed, and God didn't give a rat's ass. . . ."

"So that's where you got all that stuff about the face and voice of God?" I asked, risking an interruption.

"Got to finish." Mister John drew in a breath, exhaled with a rattling sound in this throat, and continued. "See, Wolfe had power, special power over all of us. Like a cult leader. We hated him and were afraid of him, but we followed him. Thought a lot about it all these years— the evil in him. Pure . . . like holiness in a saint. Didn't give a shit about winning medals or commendations or promotion or winning the war. Not that he wanted to lose it, uh-uh, he wanted it to go on and on. . . . Did I mention that he was on his *third* in tour?"

I shook my head.

"Next time out, Wolfe tested Salerno. Company captured a VC. Wolfe ordered Salerno to shoot him and he did. Beginning of the end for him. He . . . evolved. Shed his old skin, little by little."

For the next fifteen minutes, I listened to an account of a slow-motion massacre that left me numb. The Wolfpack killed four hundred people, civilians mostly, in six or seven months, a slaughter in which Paul Salerno became a willing and, in time, eager participant. "Wolfe was proud of him. He was Wolfe's creation, with help from the jungle. The leeches, mosquitos sucking your blood, and. . ."

"I know what it was like," I said.

"Wore away at a man. Wrecked his immune system. The soul's immune system, I mean," Mister John continued. "Salerno hated the jungle, but nothing he could do about it; hated Wolfe, but nothing he could do about him. Hated the VC because they wouldn't quit, and the farmers because they wouldn't quit, either. Leave their rice paddies and villages for a while, scared shitless of the Wolfpack, and then come right back. The Wolfpack couldn't dry up the sea! Most of all, hated himself for what he was doing, but kept right on *because* he hated it."

"That doesn't make a whole lot of sense."

"Looking for a bottom to his hatred, and one day . . . found it. Wolfpack attacked a village . . . people ran out . . . down a paddy dike. . . ." His voice beginning to falter, Mister John took another gulp from the water bottle. "One of them . . . shaved head, yellow robes. A monk. Wolfe yelled, 'Drop 'em!' and we did. We went to make sure they were dead, but the monk wasn't, and Wolfe said to Salerno, 'You know what to do,' and . . . the blood . . . the blood spreading over the yellow robes. . . . It was like an alarm gonged in Salerno's head, woke him out of a nightmare that was real. He'd killed a monk, a holy man. That's when he knew Wolfe taking orders from the devil, and since he was taking orders from Wolfe, so was he. Lost hope. Knew he could never go home. He was a short-timer by then, a month, maybe five weeks to go, but he knew he couldn't get on that plane back to The World because of what he'd seen, what he'd done. . . . What would he say to the people he knew? He wanted to die. . ."

The flood of words stopped. He gestured at the bucket and tried to get off his bed. I had to help him, clasping him by the armpits to pull him upright. To touch him, to stand so close to him was repulsive. Gripping the bedpost with one hand to steady himself, he pushed his robe aside and urinated into the makeshift chamber pot. The stream revived the dormant stench: piss, shit, and vomit testifying to more than a sickness of the body.

"So, he got his wish, he died," I said.

"But not before. . ." Mister John swayed and clutched the bamboo bedpost with both hands. "Not before. . . . Had to be done . . . Had to. . ."

The effort of telling his tale had drained his last remaining strength, and standing up must have caused what Lujan would term a postural drop in blood pressure. Before I could ask what had to be done, Mister John swooned and fell backward across the bed. Alarmed, I took him by the ankles and swung his legs so he lay straight. I looked for his wife and son, but they must have slipped away during the last hour. When I laid the back of my hand on his forehead, it felt like a freshly-ironed cloth. I took his pulse. It fluttered and stopped, fluttered and stopped. He gazed up at me, and croaked, "All this, for your ears only."

"I'm going to get the doctor," I said.

"Your ears only, you swear?"

"Yes, all right, yes, I swear."

I found a rag lying in a corner, soaked it with the remaining water, and lay it on his forehead. There was a slight leakage of blood from his nose. The nose with its prominent ridge, the slight hook at the tip, confirmed a suspicion that had been ghosting around in the back of my mind for the past half an hour. It was the change in my line of sight that jogged my memory: looking down on him rather than at him, as I had looked down at the photograph in the album Barbara Lindstrom had shown me months earlier. His aged face, his gray beard and hair and the weak light had thrown me off. I'd been listening all this time to a kind of deathbed confession. Why he'd made it in the guise of an assumed identity was impossible to know. Maybe he'd lived so long as Mister John that he believed in his own fiction. Maybe it was a way to distance himself from his own actions, speaking of them as if they'd been committed by someone else. But I didn't need to speculate why he'd chosen my ears to hear his confession: he thought or believed or imagined that I, a veteran, would understand how Paul Salerno had become someone even he did not recognize. Understanding why someone who commits a crime can sometimes tow absolution in its wake. Possibly that's what he wanted from me, and through me from the outside world; possibly he wished to absolve himself: the devil, incarnated in a charismatic psychopath named Captain Wolfe, had made Paul Salerno do the things he'd done.

These thoughts and guesses raced through my mind in seconds and brought on a drop in my own blood pressure; that is, I felt light-headed, much as I had in the temple on Wandering Souls day.

Lujan and the others were in the longhouse, asleep. I woke the doctor and whispered that Mister John had taken a sudden turn for the worse. He swung out of his bunk and rubbed his face and said in an undertone, "We'd given up on you. What's up?"

Thinking, *a lot more than you'll ever know*, I described the nosebleed, the fainting spell, the erratic pulse. Lujan dressed quickly, grabbed the rucksack containing his instruments and medications, then woke Byers and filled him in on the situation. The three of us hurried through the darkened village. My brain was hurrying, too. I had a good idea why Mister John, formerly Paul Salerno, had exiled himself to this hot, buggy, disease-ridden hermitage in the Indochina jungles; but the *how* baffled me. How had he pulled off his remarkable escape? Somehow, he'd survived the ambush that killed everyone else in the patrol; somehow, he'd taken cover, knocking out two of his teeth in the process, and remained hidden from the enemy long enough to emerge safely; somehow, he'd come upon the bodies of Chriswell and Chandler, trapped in the root system of the banyan tree. Could that have been when desertion occurred to him? Observing that Chriswell's face was unrecognizable, he'd ripped off Chriswell's dog tags and replaced them with his own. Corporal Paul Salerno would be declared killed in action, his body placed in a sealed metal coffin draped with a flag and flown back to his family in New Jersey, where he would be forever remembered as a hero who had died for his country. He'd had no way of knowing that the body would not be recovered. He would not know until, years later, Lham's hunting party reported finding the two skeletons. That coincidence must have shocked him. Why did he order the remains to be brought to the village for burial? To hide them? Maybe, but that seemed a stretch. Was it out of respect for his fallen comrades? That, too, was unlikely—he sure as hell hadn't shown Chriswell much respect.

I thought this scenario offered a plausible explanation for Mister John's implausible existence. I wanted to confront him with it and convince him to shed the pretense of his phony persona. I wanted him to tell me if my guesswork had hit the truth, or at least come close. And if it hadn't, then to reveal what the truth was. I would have to contrive a way to interview him in private; I'd made a pledge to him, and I would keep it. Like the priests he must have gone to when he was a good Catholic boy in New Jersey, his secret sins would remain with me—not for his sake, but for his sister's.

The interview never took place. He was unconscious when we arrived at the longhouse, and he remained unconscious for, oh, I can't recall how long. Lujan said it was what he had feared: Dengue Shock Syndrome. Mister John's wife and green-eyed son, along with Lham, came to his bedside. No one had summoned them; how they'd known the crisis had come was another riddle. Mister John's blood pressure plummeted from ninety over sixty to seventy over forty and finally to zero. His eyes stilled, his mouth opened, expelling a last breath, as fetid as the jungles he had hated.

"Father die?" the son asked.

Lujan felt for a pulse and nodded. "I'm sorry. *Sin Loi.*"

"He told me that he thought he'd be gone by morning," I said. "Like a premonition."

"Don't go mystical again," said Lujan, wiping blood from Mister John's nostrils and gums with gauze patches.

"He must have told you more than that," Byers said. "You had a long talk. What did he say?"

“Not much I could make sense of,” I answered, explaining that he’d been semi-delirious, rambling and babbling. I met the captain’s gaze with a fairly good imitation of candor in mine.

Early in the morning, when it was still dark, Glun, Lham, and two other men wrapped the corpse in a reed mat. A stretcher composed of two long poles lashed with rope to shorter cross-pieces lay on the floor. By this time, the rest of the team had learned of Mister John’s death and gathered outside the longhouse, hoping for a glimpse of him. They didn’t get one—the mat covered his face. He looked like a mummy. He was to be buried in the village cemetery at daybreak, said the village chief through Trinh. Byers whipped his head side to side as if he were shaking water out of an ear. The body of the first and only missing American to have been found alive must be flown to Hanoi and eventually to the United States, where it would be kept in a morgue until his family could be located and notified. Trinh was at some pains translating. Glun’s cork-colored face wore an expression of amused indulgence, such as might be bestowed on an idiot child. He apprised Byers that it was the Montagnard custom to bury their dead as quickly as possible. And Mister John *was* theirs, he’d been initiated into the tribe. As for his family—with a movement of his chin, Glun indicated Mister John’s son and wife, sitting motionless against a wall—his family was here.

“He has a point, captain,” Lujan said.

Prine seconded him. We were in uncharted waters, she said, with an authority in her low, calm voice. No procedures, no protocols to follow. The problem was beyond our pay grade.

The captain ran a hand through his brush cut. “And if Chriswell’s relatives are located, what do we tell them? That we stood by while he was put in the ground in the middle of nowhere?”

“It’s for the attaché and the embassy to deal with,” she replied as a voice cried in my head: *He’s not Chriswell*!

Mister John was interred at dawn to chants and a great clanging of gongs. We attended the ceremony. Everyone in the village was there, perhaps two hundred people. As the grave was covered over, Byers looked anxious, even a little scared, imagining—so I guessed—that he would be reprimanded by the Joint Command or by the attaché or both. I was anxious and scared myself, for different reasons.

The helicopter that was to have medevacked Mister John instead flew the seven of us back to base camp. The captain raised the attaché on the satphone, and gave him an abbreviated account of our discovery. We broke camp, packed up, and returned to Danang. From there, Vietnam Airways whisked us and our artifacts, in sealed evidence bags, to Hanoi. The attaché and some very serious gentlemen belonging to "TC2" escorted us to the Metropole. We were assigned rooms on the same floor and instructed not to leave the hotel, the serious gentlemen taking up posts in the corridor to make sure we stayed put. Prine and Byers went off with the attaché to the embassy.

That evening, the captain assembled the team in a conference room. He was accompanied by a Vietnamese general in uniform and the attaché, a slender man wearing a white shirt with no tie. They informed us that the discovery of John T. Chriswell had been classified, a strict gag order imposed on all of us.

"What we don't want or need is a media carnival, nutballs going ballistic on the internet," the attaché said in a tone both mild and firm. He tilted his head at the general, indicating that "we" included the Vietnamese government as well as the government of the United States. "To repeat, it's classified. Meaning none of you can say word one about this to anyone outside this room. You do and you'll be liable for criminal prosecution. Questions?"

There weren't any. I looked at the wall, wishing it were a window.

Barbara Lindstrom invited me to attend the memorial service with her and her family at Riverside National Cemetery. It's a lovely, pastoral place: artificial lakes, fountains, black marble monuments to the missing and the dead, and a wide, manicured meadow where small flags flutter over flat stone markers, thousands of them. Her brother's looked like this:

SALERNO

PAUL F. CPL. U.S. ARMY

VIETNAM

1947–1969

LOVED THEN, NOW, ALWAYS.

A squad of soldiers who hadn't been born when Salerno went to war fired a rifle salute with admirable precision, a bugler blew taps. Altogether a fine and fitting ceremony on a fine and fitting California afternoon. Barbara cried, but she told me they were more tears of happiness than of sorrow. *I don't care if it's a rib, a finger, just something, anything I can put in the ground and say, There he is...* All she had to put in the ground was a sealed transfer case the size of a jewelry box that had been presented to her in Hawaii. It contained two teeth, a premolar and a molar, the latter with a restoration. My surmise that they'd been Salerno's had proven correct: The lab at Hickam Field had compared them to his dental records. They matched. I don't know what I would have done, what I would have said to Barbara if they hadn't. Feel free to condemn me for withholding the truth from her. There are some things in life which ought not to be looked into too deeply. As far as she and the world were concerned, Corporal Paul Salerno had died a hero forty years before.

There is an old saying that a conspiracy of two is safe if one is dead.

In a sense, I had conspired with Mister John to keep his secrets both to spare his sister needless pain but also to pay him a debt for reminding me of something I'd forgotten. I'd begun to look back on my war experiences with a certain nostalgia, to see them through a haze as it were, forgetting, or ignoring, war's power to maim and mutilate more than mere flesh and bone.

Close to a year had passed when Martha Prine phoned—she and Byers, now Major Byers, were in LA and leaving soon on another expedition. Could they stop by for a visit? Sure, I said, assuming they weren't making a social call; even in good traffic, it's a two-and-a-half-hour drive from LA to San Diego.

The afternoon was breezy and warm. Delia brought Diet Cokes with lime twists and we sat down at a patio table in my modest backyard. In her cargo pants and quick-dry shirt, sinewy, suntanned Prine looked like an Outward Bound instructor. Byers, wearing a polo shirt and khaki slacks and golf shoes, appeared to have come off the links.

"We thought we'd let you know that the lab got results from the DNA tests on the skulls," Prine said, after we'd dispensed with the usual How-Have-You-Beens. "Took a long time. They were in pretty bad shape, in the ground forty years, handled by other people."

"And we located Chandler's family," Byers added. "But not Chriswell's. He was an only child of a father who was an only child and he's gone and so is Chriswell's mother. We're trying to find a cousin but so far, no luck."

He folded his hands across his stomach and squinted at me. I sipped my coke.

"Didn't you tell us that back in sixty-nine you took their dog tags?" he asked.

"My squad leader took them."

"Right. And Salerno's tags were on the body with the head wounds?"

"That's how I remember it."

Prine frowned. "We got a DNA sample off that skull and compared it with a swab we'd got from Barbara Lindstrom. We thought it would be nice if we could give her more than a couple of teeth, but no match. Could your memory have been wrong?"

I shrugged. "Maybe. Did you tell her that the samples didn't match?"

"I didn't. The teeth were enough, the teeth would have to do. Our Mister John showed you a set of dog tags he'd kept in a box, and those belonged to Chriswell."

"You two are driving at something," I said, continuing to play dumb. "What is it?"

"We're trying to keep our own records straight and accurate," answered Prine. "We've had too many problems with misidentifications. We'd like to be sure of who was buried in that Montagnard village. And, you might say, what brought him there."

I didn't say anything.

"I've done some deeper digging," Byers said into my silence. "A PFC John Chriswell was in that patrol. He and Salerno and Chandler did belong to some black ops outfit, like I'd thought. They did some pretty nasty shit. More like terrorists than soldiers. Their C.O., a Captain Jonas Wolfe, was killed a week or so before the objects of our search went on the Body-Not-Recovered list. One of his own men fragged him. Or more than one. . . . There was an Article 32 underway. . ."

That jolted me. *It had to be done.* The second to last words I'd heard Salerno speak. It became instantly clear that guilt and shame had not been his sole motive for exiling himself. More than a deserter, he'd been a fugitive, in flight from an investigation that was bound to charge him with murdering his commanding officer.

"Something the matter?" asked Captain-now-Major Byers. My shock must have shown.

"No. You were saying, an Article 32. . ."

"Nothing ever came of it; it went up the chain of command and was quashed. I think I know why."

"Because an investigation into this Captain Wolfe's fragging might have expanded into the actions of his troops?"

"It's why I couldn't find any records back when I started researching this case." Byers's gaze drifted to my backyard fence. "They sat in a file drawer somewhere until they were shredded, almost everything—the Article 32, Wolfe's after-action reports. That was in November or December of sixty-nine, right after My Lai made the front pages. The last thing the army needed was another scandal about American troops massacring people."

"You're saying that Chriswell. . ."

"I'm not saying a thing. Let me try it from another angle, a review of facts, okay?"

"Okay."

"Fact one—You told us that you and your squad found five bodies out there, that you and the squad leader retrieved dog tags from two of the bodies. Salerno's and Chandler's. No mention of a sixth body or a Chriswell. But we now know—Fact two—that Chriswell was with the patrol. Fact three— His dog tags were in the possession of Mister John. Fact four—the skull you identified as Salerno's turns out not to be his. So, whose was it? Could that be John Chriswell?"

"Without a DNA sample to compare, we may never know," Prine interjected. "Dental records are no good, either, the teeth were so smashed up."

Byers's fingers tapped a ragged drumbeat on my patio table. "Teeth. Lujan confirmed that Mister John was missing two teeth. He didn't get a good look at which ones, his mind was on treating the guy's fever. But we're guessing they were a premolar and a molar. What do you think?"

"Is this conversation going to be classified?"

"Nope. But I can promise it won't go beyond us."

"Then I'd say your guess is right."

"You were the last one to talk to him, and it's another guess that whatever he said to you wasn't just delirious babble?"

"He told me a lot, none of it pretty, but never anything about fragging Captain Wolfe," I answered, relieved to shed the burden I'd been carrying for so long. "I think he was about to, but he collapsed before he could."

They both nodded solemnly.

"How did you know the teeth would match Salerno's dental records?" asked Prine.

"I didn't. I was pretty sure, but I didn't know. Took a chance."

"Yeah, you did," Byers said, in an accusatory way. "You should have said something to us. You had reason for not doing that?"

I gave him a sharp look and told him my reason. I had two, but kept one, the purely personal one, to myself.

"You didn't believe his sister, a grown woman, could handle the truth?" asked Prine. "A bit patronizing, don't you think?"

"Here's the truth—Salerno was a war criminal, not the war hero his sister thinks he was. I wasn't going to be the one to tell her that, I wasn't going to tell her that her brother had been alive all this time, that he'd deserted, turned his back on his country and on . . . her. But if you want to, hey, go ahead. Then your records will be all nice and tidy and straight and accurate."

Prine smiled and extended her hand across the table. "This has all been off the record," she said.

A few days after the visit, she emailed me a photograph of a grave in the national cemetery in Hawaii, where a broken skull believed but not known to be the remains of John Chriswell had been buried. The grave marker read: UNKNOWN. Gone, I thought, gone with no acknowledgment that he'd ever breathed the sweet air. Had he, too, been corrupted by Captain Wolfe? Had he taken part in the fragging? Unanswerable questions. Still, I hoped his soul was not among those wandering the earth, hoped his interment, despite its anonymity, sufficed to give him rest.

A NEAR-DEATH EXPERIENCE

He fell in love with her after he died. Lambert fell in love easily (married three times; about a dozen pre-, post-, and extra-marital affairs), partly because he loved being in love, but mostly because he was searching for the Great Romance that would endlessly arouse and consume his desires and never fade into mere affection: the fire that, feeding on itself, could never be extinguished. When a marriage or a relationship aged, as they all do, its kisses wilting into smooches, its hot embraces cooling into hugs, he fell out of love. To those who thought of him charitably, he was a hopeless romantic; to the less charitable, a seventeen-year-old in a fifty-seven-year-old's body.

His quest for the Great Romance sprang from his loathing of the commonplace and his need to live intensely—the very same loathing and need that had led him to become a wildlife photographer. He'd spent much of his adult life in remote places, lying in wait, sometimes for weeks, for the perfect shot of small creatures, like spiders, rare ones, like the bezoar ibex, and dangerous ones, like leopards, grizzly bears, and Cape buffalo. He preferred the dangerous ones—they were naturally photogenic and their ability to kill him had the same effect as an addictive drug. The thrill of capturing them on film begetting the compulsion to do it again and again and again.

He'd won many awards and was much in demand, commanding top fees from magazines like *Audubon* and *National Geographic.* He was on assignment for the latter in Kenya when he met Marlene Ryder. She caught the eye of most men, and she caught Lambert's the moment he first saw her, sitting on the tailgate of a pickup truck, her tanned legs crossed at the ankles. She looked to be in her late twenties, dressed in baggy safari shorts, a light green shirt, a baseball cap, and buff desert boots with dirty white socks showing an inch or two above their tops. It was hardly an attractive outfit, but she did not need one with those long legs of hers and that straight nose and finely cut chin. Her coal black hair tumbled out from her cap and over sloping shoulders, and her sunglasses were hooked by one temple to her shirt. Even from a distance, Lambert could make out the color of her eyes—violet—and he immediately thought of Elizabeth Taylor. Black hair, violet eyes.

When Keyes, the biologist in charge of the expedition, introduced her—this was in the expedition's base camp on the Tsavo River—he described her as "my grad assistant," to which she responded, "Actually, I'm his *confrere*," exaggerating the French pronunciation for comic effect, to show that her use of it wasn't a pretense.

"Pleasure to meet you, Mister Lambert," she said, bathing him in a radiant smile. "Ron has told me all about you, best in the business, he said. Is he right?"

"I defer to his judgment. And it's Doug."

She shook his hand—a businesslike handshake, firm and forthright. "Okie-doke, Doug. Look forward to working with you."

In two weeks, he would die and rise from death into love; but at that initial meeting, he felt nothing more than a mild attraction. He was too jet-lagged and travel-worn—New York to Amsterdam, Amsterdam to Nairobi, Nairobi to Tsavo by bush plane, followed by a bone-rattling Land Rover ride from the airstrip to camp, its green tents pitched on a low bluff overlooking the river and the thornbush plains beyond. Victoria Watson, the outfitter, had driven him herself rather than delegating the job to one of her "boys," as she called her drivers, cooks, and porters. A weathered white Kenyan in her fifties, Victoria retained some of the mannerisms and vocabulary of her colonialist forbears, though she did so from custom rather than any sense of racial superiority. But she left no doubt that she was the *memsahib* and they her employees, as when she snapped orders to two of them to carry Lambert's baggage to his tent: a duffel containing his clothes, two metal suitcases with his digital and film cameras, long lenses, and rolls of slide and color film inside.

Two events deepened his feelings for Marlene, softening him up, as it were, for love's final assault. The first happened two days after he met her. They left camp before dawn, Marlene at the wheel of a Land Rover whose best days were ten thousand miles behind it. She was hunting for a black-maned lion; if she found one, she said, her plan was to conduct field experiments to determine if dark-haired males were dominant over blondes. This would be "the last data point" for her doctoral dissertation, the purpose of which was to answer the question: Why do lions have manes?

Lambert grunted "uh-huh." He didn't consider the question one of the great ones confronting humanity; might as well ask: Why did people have pubic hair? Although he'd photographed many scientific expeditions, he lacked a scientific temperament. He wasn't interested in discovering why things were the way they were, preferring the inexplicable to remain inexplicable. His purpose, his joy, lay in arresting the wildness, the majesty, and above all the mystery of the natural world with the click of a shutter. As for lions, it was their lethal beauty that excited him. He loved to watch them on a stalk, bellies scraping the ground, eyes focused on their prey, muscles moving under their buff brown hides like water under a taut mat.

"So what kind of experiments? How do you find out if one lion is dominant over another?" he asked just to make conversation.

"With dummies," she answered. He liked her husky voice; it reminded him of another bygone movie star, Lauren Bacall. "Ron has two life-size dummy lions, one with a dark mane, the other with a light-colored one. We set them up, then we play different kinds of roars"—twitching her head at the loud speakers and recording device in the back seat— "to draw real lions in and we observe how they react to the fakes."

"And. . . ?"

"Well, there's two features in a mane, its length and its color. We've already found out that lionesses prefer bushy manes, a sign of health. Are they're really turned on by black, bushy ones? Does the Latin lover win out over the Scandinavian? But here's the thing—manes are a liability, like wearing a parka in the summer, and that's why we're here in Tsavo. Because it's way hotter here than in the Serengeti, the males have short manes, buzz cuts, so we can factor out length in the dominance question and zoom in on color. If I can find a dark one and run the experiment. . . . Wow, that'll be it!"

All of this struck Lambert as, well, hair-splitting, but her enthusiasm was catching. "You'll be Marlene Ryder, PhD."

"Not right away. I have to write the dissertation, defend it. I'm really lucky to have Ron as my advisor. The world's foremost expert on the African lion."

"The heir to George Schaller," Lambert said. It had crossed his mind that she and Keyes might have a relationship beyond the professional. He hoped not. The grad student and the prof? A pathetic cliché.

"You and he go back a long way, he told me," Marlene said.

"More than ten years."

A gray light washed away the morning stars. Ahead, a broad plateau of yellow grass, speckled with acacia and baobab trees, spread toward the Chyulu Hills. The backs of Cape buffalo, looking like charcoal-colored boulders, humped out of the grass in the far distance. A zebra herd filed across the road a hundred yards or so in front of the Land Rover. Marlene stopped to let them pass.

"And so the day's nature documentary begins," she said. "Tourist Africa. Nothing like the Africa Africans have to live with."

Leaning out the window, Lambert trained a long lens on the zebra and shot a few frames to loosen up for the morning's work.

"Malaria and Ebola and AIDs," Marlene was saying. "Civil wars and dictators and what just might be the most corrupt governments on the planet, except maybe for Russia."

"We might be catching up. I sat next to a guy from Zimbabwe on the flight to Nairobi. He said he was happy that the US elected Trump. I asked him why and he said, 'Now you Americans will know what it's like to have an African president.'"

She laughed. "Hey, there's a truth-teller."

They drove on, the Land Rover trailing a funnel of salmon-colored dust. Stopping again, on a low rise, Marlene glanced at the GPS mounted on the dashboard.

"We have arrived. Ogeto spotted a pride right around here the other day." She pointed at a thornbush jungle across a grassy meadow, about a quarter-mile wide, on the right side of the road. "So now we'll try to draw them out and see if a blackie is among them."

As she reached into the back seat for the loudspeaker her shirt opened at the top, providing a glimpse of her cleavage. Lambert turned quickly away, so she didn't catch him gawking. A middle-aged man leering at a young woman was also a pathetic cliché, and he did not think of himself as pathetic or prone to clichés.

Marlene opened the door and climbed onto the roof and secured the speaker to the roof rack with bungee cord. Oh, to be that flexible, that nimble again, he thought. A pair of wires dropped down, dangling past the passenger side window.

"Hey, Doug," she called from above, "do you mind plugging the power cord into the cigarette lighter and the jack into the recorder?"

He didn't mind at all. Marlene then settled back into the driver's seat and flipped the recorder's power switch. A series of deep grunts, followed by a spine-chilling roar, then another, blasted from the speaker toward the thornbush thickets.

"That's an invading male announcing himself. A challenge," she said.

She and Lambert watched and waited. Nothing happened. She tried again, cranking up the volume. He noticed movement in the distant thickets. In a moment, just as the roar sounded a third time, a small elephant herd—three cows and as many calves—shambled into clear view. The lead cow, the herd matriarch, whirled and stood staring intently at the Land Rover, her ears flapping like giant, gray signal flags. Their message was unequivocal. Then she charged.

Marlene said, "Oh, shit," jumped outside, swung herself onto the roof, and got back into the car, tossing the bullhorn into the rear seat and starting the engine in one swift movement. The matriarch was already better than halfway across the meadow, running stiff-legged, head down, trunk tucked between her short, blunt tusks. Three tons of angry elephant coming straight on. In a few seconds, she would ram them broadside. Lambert, thrilled and terrified at the same time, shot a dozen burst frames in the time it took for Marlene to engage the gears and floor the accelerator. The Land Rover wasn't designed for a fast pickup; it seemed to take forever to get to twenty-five, the matriarch in pursuit until the car reached forty and left her behind. Looking back, Lambert saw her standing in the road, swinging her trunk in indignation. Marlene eased up on the gas and laughed a laugh that sounded like wind chimes.

"There is nothing so stimulating as to be shot at without effect," she said.

"Winston Churchill, when he was covering the Boer War. You were great. If you'd been a little slower getting that thing off the roof and us out of the way . . . You weren't scared?"

"No time to be." Marlene tossed him a quick glance. A wild light sparkled in her purple-blue eyes. "Stimulated, I'd say."

Their adventure was the main topic of dinner conversation in the camp's dining hall, which wasn't a hall but an open-sided structure with a thatch roof supported by wood beams and posts. Kudu and buffalo horns hung from the posts, propane lanterns from the beams.

"So . . . your lion imitation did work, only it fooled the wrong species," Victoria Watson said. She hoisted a bottle of red, and poured into each glass. "A damned good South African, as good as anything the bloody French turn out."

"I disagree," said Ogeto. He was a research biologist from the University of Nairobi, a colleague who'd joined the expedition. "Not about the wine. About the elephant mistaking the Land Rover for a lion. Elephants are intelligent." Tapping his half-bald skull. "Somali poachers are in the park, and poachers drive vehicles."

"I thought it was Toyotas, not Land Rovers" Victoria said, archly.

"I am sure make and model make no difference." Ogeto sipped his wine. "This *is* very good. The elephant mistook our friends for poachers because she has seen *her* friends shot for their ivory."

"Whatever she thought we were, that big mama was mightily pissed off," said Marlene, scrubbed and showered and shampooed, her hair lustrous in the lanterns' subdued glow. "That was no bluff charge. Doug got pictures of it. Why don't you show us, Doug?" Motioning at his camera bag.

"I'd have to develop them first," he said.

A perplexed expression came over her face.

"Doug's a bit of a Luddite," Keyes said. "Just like there's audiophiles, he's a filmophile."

"You shoot with *film*?"

She sounded both amazed and amused, as if he were an antediluvian crank who wrote letters instead of tweets. He replied, "As much as possible."

"Why?"

"Mostly it's because with analog you have to catch the moment and the mood, you have to have a sense of timing and space and light. Analog transmits the emotion of a picture like digital can't, no matter how much you fiddle with it afterward. Because it's just you and the moment and the camera in your hands."

"Wow, you're like what? A mystic?" Marlene said, raising her eyebrows. He noticed that the left had a more pronounced arch than the right, and that her lower lip was thicker than it should be—asymmetries that enhanced rather than diminished her beauty. He had a sudden, wholly unexpected urge to kiss her.

The second event occurred on a very hot afternoon. Lambert and Marlene were parked in an acacia grove bordering a deep drift, glassing a pride bedded down in tall grass about fifty yards away. Only their backs showed through the long grass, and now and then, the lazy flick of a tail shooing flies.

"There's just one thing more boring than watching lions and that's being a lion," she said after an hour during which absolutely nothing happened. "They spend three-fourths of their time doing what they're doing now."

"The other fourth is pretty lively, though," Lambert said.

"But I like them. They're great enforcers of social democracy. You could be the Queen of England, the President of the USA, the world's most gorgeous supermodel, a Nobel Prize winner, and all you'd be to a lion is a source of protein."

"Never thought of it like that. So, how long have you been a lion watcher?"

"Close to a year now. I love it, looking for lions is like a treasure hunt, but a lot of times, listening for hours for the beep of a radio collar or playing hyena calls blasting in your ears can drive you nuts."

"What's in the future? After you get the doctorate? Teaching?"

"Thanks, but no thanks. The last thing on earth I want to do is to be stuck on a campus. Academia is a bore, too. I see myself in wildlife conservation, in the field, traveling the world. The wild parts of it. What's left of them."

A kindred spirit, he thought. He squelched an impulse to ask if marriage and children figured into her plans. Lambert hoped not. He had no kids of his own; they were an impediment. He worried that he might have offended Marlene earlier, on the drive from camp. She'd described the studies she and Keyes had made of Serengeti lions: shooting them with tranquilizer darts, taking blood samples for DNA analysis, inserting tubes into their rectums for fecal samples, fitting tracking collars to their necks.

"Glad I wasn't there to see that," he'd said.

"Oh? Why?'

The picture of a lion drugged into unconsciousness, plastic tubes shoved up its ass, collared like a dog, troubled him, he'd answered. It robbed what was arguably the most iconic beast on earth of its inherent dignity. It would be more respectful to kill one with a rifle. She hit the brakes and looked him straight in the eye.

"Are you saying that what we do is *disrespectful*? You should ask Mr. Leo. What'll it be? A tranquilizer dart or a bullet through the heart? How else are we going to learn anything about them?"

"Why do we need to learn about them?" he countered.

"You really are a mystic," she batted back. "We need to learn about them for the same reason we need to learn about anything. Otherwise, we'd still be in caves, sacrificing virgins because we think the gods are pissed off."

"Maybe they are," Lambert said, and laughed at himself, averting a quarrel. He did not want a quarrel. His so far one-sided relationship with Marlene had matured into admiration: she was as bright as she was good-looking, and as the encounter with the raging elephant had shown, cool-headed and brave.

"I'm going to move up on them a little," she said. "See if I can wake them up."

She turned the ignition key, producing a click. A second try had the same result.

"Shit! I don't get it. The battery is less than a month old."

Lambert suggested a loose cable as the problem and asked if there was a tool kit on board. In the back, under the seat.

The kit consisted of no more than one screwdriver and one socket wrench. He did not relish getting out of the vehicle with a pride of lions just fifty yards away. At the same time, the seventeen-year-old in his fifty-seven-year-old body was eager to impress Marlene with his nerve and competence.

Taking the wrench, he raised the hood and tested the cables' snugness with his fingers. They felt tight enough, but he gave each hex nut a quarter turn to make sure and told Marlene to try again. Another sickening click. Camp was ten miles away, cellphone service was nonexistent. Two sources of protein hiking ten miles unarmed through lion country. . . . Lambert closed the hood as softly as possible, at a loss what to do; then he noticed that the road led into and across the drift, sloping down twenty feet at about a thirty-degree angle.

"I'm going to give it a push downhill," he said to Marlene. "You know what to do?"

"Put it in neutral, pop the clutch as soon as it's rolling."

The Land Rover was heavier than he'd anticipated. It took all his strength to get it moving and then to push it to the edge of the drift, where a slight rise in the ground stopped it dead. Marlene climbed out, took a shovel strapped to the roof rack, and began to hack at the clods of dirt blocking the front wheels. She and Lambert took turns, one shoveling while the other kept an eye on the dozing lions.

"I'll give you hand pushing," she said when they were done.

Leaving the door on the driver's side open, she put her shoulder into the frame as Lambert pushed from the rear. He pushed hard as he could, and tripped on an exposed tree root just as the car began to roll downhill. Stumbling after it, arms whirling to keep from falling on his face, he saw Marlene hop onto the running board and leap inside, supple and quick as a gymnast swinging on parallel bars. An instant later came the wonderful cough and rumble of the engine starting and her cry of "Yeehah!"

He ran down to the Land Rover, idling at the bottom of the drift, and climbed in beside her.

"Was that awesome or what?" she said, her face flushed with exhilaration. She high-fived him and blew him a kiss.

A feeling of camaraderie sprang up between them. They had faced dangers and difficulties together, and together they had overcome them. In fact, he was already in love, only he didn't know it. Even if he did, he would not have expressed it. Nearly twice her age, he was wary of making a fool of himself. She was a hard read besides. Focused on her project, to the exclusion of everything else, there didn't seem to be room in her life for a relationship other than professional. But she'd begun to show him signs of an innocent affection—the light touch on his forearm or shoulder, bumping her hip into his when he said something funny. A couple times, as they sat talking during stakeouts for a black-maned lion, she cracked a window into her personal life—raised in Portland, Oregon, worked her way through undergrad as a sales clerk in a jewelry store, hiked up Kilimanjaro with a Brit she'd dated while working on Keyes's lion projects in Tanzania, broke up with him before coming to Kenya. That was all, the sketchiest of sketches.

As the days passed without sighting her quarry, Marlene grew irritable and frustrated. Concern for his student's project, as well as her state of mind, led Keyes to enlist the services of a man Lambert came to call The Invasive Weed, as if referring to him by his given name, Martin Beech, conferred a respect he did not deserve. Beech the Leech—the nickname he eventually settled on—was a type of conman he'd run into before. They popped up in the world's remote corners, which provided environments congenial to whatever hustles they might be working. Beech had passed himself off to park authorities as an authentic scientist engaged in important work—proving a novel theory that Tsavo lions were a distinct subspecies directly descended from the European cave lions of prehistoric times. He'd persuaded or bribed—most likely bribed—the officials to grant him a permit to drive off-road anywhere in the park—a privilege denied everyone else, Keyes included—and to provide living quarters, at a ridiculously low rent, for him and his girlfriend, Vanity.

Keyes and Ogeto discovered him on a visit to park headquarters to request that the superintendent report any sightings his rangers made of dark-maned lions. Beech happened to be there, renewing his permit, and volunteered his assistance. He knew Tsavo like his own backyard, all eight-thousand square miles of it. Keyes wasn't taken in by him, recognizing him as a charlatan eager to attach himself to a legitimate scientific endeavor, but Beech's familiarity with the park's geography overrode his reservations. He invited Beech and Vanity to dinner that night.

Lambert and Marlene disliked him instantly. He talked, almost incessantly, in an adenoidal South African twang, and the less he knew about a subject the more he talked about it. When Marlene inquired what evidence he had for his notion that the lions of Tsavo were living fossils, he replied, "Ivadince? Ya iver seen them two maneatin' critters they got stuffed in the mew-see-um in Chicago? Bald as bowlin' balls, just like the lions ya see pinted on cave walls in the Palolithic era. No manes at all! There's ya ivadince!" Vanity gazed at him worshipfully as he mouthed this drivel. Lambert could not imagine them having sex—the picture would have been repulsive if it weren't so ludicrous. She was close to six feet tall, he a head shorter; her hair was luxuriant and cinnamon brown, his sparse and gray; her eyes were denim blue and candid, his, the color of dirty dishwater and evasive.

Evidently, Beech the Leech considered the dinner invitation open-ended; he and Vanity showed up in camp the next evening, and the next, and the next. The alleged purpose of these visits was to report on what he'd found during his daylight forays—generally nothing useful. Vanity was fiercely protective of him, shooting darts at anyone who challenged his brilliant theories. She reminded Lambert of a daughter fiercely protective of an eccentric father whom she cherishes for qualities other people cannot see or find insufferable. On the fourth night, the couple moved into camp—"so's we can bitter coordinate our activities," he told Keyes. This was too much for Victoria, who demanded a 10 percent hike in her fees if she was expected to feed two mouths more than originally agreed upon. It was too much for Lambert, whose dislike of the man matured into hatred when Beech, spotting Lambert's single malt as they sat by the campfire, exclaimed, "The Macallen! Now ya talkin'," and helped himself to a jigger. And it was far too much for Marlene.

Lambert overheard her scolding Keyes later on, after everyone else had turned in for the night. "How could you have asked that fraud to join us? . . . working my ass off for my doctorate . . . that idiot with his nutball ideas . . . eating our food, talking bullshit . . . it's insulting. . . "

Keyes murmured something Lambert could not make out.

"Not good enough!" Marlene said. "Tomorrow. You tell them to leave first thing tomorrow!"

But when morning came, Keyes failed to expel the unwanted guests. He didn't even try. He hated confrontations. Lambert gulped his malaria pill with breakfast coffee and left camp with one of Victoria's drivers to shoot some landscapes.

That evening, as usual, everyone assembled around the campfire for drinks before dinner. Marlene sat in her camp chair, arms crossed tightly over her abdomen, as if she had a bellyache, and stared blankly at the flames. Lambert sipped his scotch. Calculating that Beech would be able to locate the bottle by smell, as a dog can sniff out an exposed plate of ground beef, he'd locked the bottle in one of the camera cases in his tent.

Beech was nattering on about the time, more than twenty years ago, when he'd been a technical advisor for the film about the Tsavo maneaters, *The Ghost and the Darkness.*

"Me and Val Kilmer was drinkin' mates, we'd tip a few together when the day's shootin' was over and done."

"His whiskey or yours?" Lambert asked.

Beech ignored the jab, or wasn't aware of it. "Seen that movie? Val played Colonel Patterson."

"I did. Don't remember seeing your name in the credits."

"Oh, c'mon. Must've been five hundred people worked on it. How could you remember who was who this many years down the road?"

"How about Vilmos Zsigmond?"

"Who's that?"

"Friend of mine."

"He was in the crew, this Vilmos bloke?"

"The cinematographer," said Lambert, feeling the nasty thrill of a prosecutor who traps a lying witness. "I'd think that if you and the star were drinking buddies, you'd know who shot the damn movie."

Vanity rose, literally, to her boyfriend's defense, springing from her chair to glare at Lambert. "Just what are you implying?"

"That he never had anything to do that movie. It's bullshit, like ninety percent of what comes out of his mouth."

"You're despicable."

"All right, you three," said Victoria. "Let's not have any unpleasantness."

Beech paid her no attention, and making an unsuccessful attempt to look menacing, turned to Lambert. "I don't know who you think you are, but. . ."

"You should leave, the both of you," Lambert interrupted, calmly. "You're not welcome here anymore, so how about you pack up and shove off."

He didn't know what had come over him. He hadn't planned to provoke an argument, nor to give Beech and Vanity an eviction notice. But he was glad he did when he saw that Marlene had snapped out of her sulk and was sitting up straight, looking at him with, he hoped, admiration.

Beech stood, blinking as if someone were shining a flashlight into his face. "So, who's the boss here, you or him?" he said to Keyes, and receiving no reply, put the question to Victoria, who also didn't answer. "'Pears to be he is, he's the boss, speakin' for all of you," he said, and snorted derisively.

Camp morale improved just minutes after he and Vanity drove away. The five people remaining trooped into dinner. Eland steaks were served. Victoria thanked Lambert for ridding them of the Invasive Weed, though she added that he could have gone about it more diplomatically.

"Diplomacy wouldn't work on him," Marlene said. "His type needs a crack on the head."

Her approval was all Lambert cared about. He sat down across from her and next to Victoria, who filled each glass with Kanonkop Pinotage, her favorite South African red. Raising hers, she said, "In any case, good riddance to bad rubbish. Cheers, everyone."

"Cheers," Lambert echoed and took a healthy swallow.

Then, out of nowhere, the table and everyone seated at it seemed to tip to one side. He reached out his hand to grab hold of Victoria, to stop himself from falling, but her tanned, seamed face was the last thing he saw before being catapulted to the arched entrance of some magnificent building. Unsure of what was happening, he looked in through the building's palladium windows, and through these windows shone an ineffable light, the most sublime thing he'd ever beheld. There were people inside, dozens of them, appearing as a single, grayish-blue mass, not one of whom he could identify by name, yet he knew in some indescribable way that they were friends and relatives who had died. All sense of time had ceased. No past, no future, only an eternal present as one person stepped out of the crowd, a featureless silhouette that he nonetheless recognized as his paternal grandmother, Rosalind, his favorite relation, and she was bidding him, "Welcome, welcome," though she wasn't speaking the words but communicating the idea, the essence, as it were, of welcomeness. She and the glorious light flooded him with an intense bliss such as he'd never known. He was about to pass through the entrance when he heard. . .

"There's no pulse. . . . He hasn't got a pulse!"

It was Marlene. He was looking straight into her face and she was sobbing. Then he felt a weight on his chest, someone was pressing down on it, relaxing, pressing again. Keyes. Keyes straddling him as he lay on the floor, administering CPR.

"Wait, yes!" Marlene cried out. "I feel it now, his pulse is back!"

Keyes and Ogeto, each taking him under an arm, lifted him into a chair and the bliss spilled out of him instantly. He felt groggy and dejected.

The withdrawal of that unutterable beatitude, so swiftly, so completely, that is what depressed him.

"Doug? Are you with us?" Keyes said, softly slapping him, as a cornerman does to a fighter after a bad round.

Lambert nodded.

"You gave us a scare. One second, you're drinking your wine, next second, your eyes go blank, I mean no light in them, second after that, you groan and keel over."

"And we are all shouting to you," Ogeto added. "'Doug, Doug,' we are shouting but no response."

"No pulse, no heartbeat for maybe a minute, maybe two," Marlene said, her eyes dry now. "You weren't breathing."

"You were . . . like . . . dead," said Keyes.

"Two minutes? That was all?" Lambert asked.

Marlene answered, "Two max."

"It felt like hours, days," he said for lack of better terms. In that state of temporal suspension, conventional measures of time meant nothing. "I went somewhere."

"Yes, the floor," said Victoria in her no-nonsense, old Colonial manner of speaking.

"I saw my grandmother. She's been dead twenty years."

Victoria patted him on the arm. "Yes, of course, dear boy."

She rose and went behind the bar, fetched a satellite phone, and called the Flying Doctor Service in Nairobi. Lambert, emerging from his daze, heard her give his name and a description of what had happened to the desk nurse, who then asked a series of questions. Victoria relayed them to him: Did he have a history of heart trouble? No. Food allergies? No. A bee sting, a snake bite? No and no. Had he been drinking alcohol? Yes. A couple ounces of whiskey, a sip of wine. How about water? No. What medications was he taking, if any? Only Lariam, once a week.

"Lariam! Didn't I tell you before you came out here never to take that drug?" Keyes scolded.

Victoria shushed him with a brusque wave. A long discussion ensued between her and the nurse. Lambert could hear only one side of the conversation. She ended the call and said that the Service didn't think his condition serious enough to warrant the risk of landing a small aircraft on an unlighted airstrip at night. He'd apparently suffered a Lariam-induced seizure, aggravated by dehydration, resulting in a brief cardiac arrest. The Flying Doctors saw cases like his a few times each year.

"Get a good night's rest, and if you're feeling well in the morning, I'll drive you up to Nairobi hospital for a checkup. One of us should keep an eye on you tonight, in case of another seizure."

Lambert replied with a nod. Marlene brought him a bottle of water. He drank half of it in a single swallow.

"Gonna put the patient to bed," said Keyes, and escorted him to his tent, once again reprimanding him for taking Lariam against his advice. "That drug ought to be outlawed."

"It wasn't a seizure, Keyes. And it wasn't dehydration. I went somewhere. I saw my grandmother and she was welcoming me to wherever it was."

"Sure. Right. I knew a guy in Tanzania who was on Larium and woke up one night and saw a black-winged angel sitting at the foot of his bed. He swore it was the angel of death. Get some sleep. Doctor's orders."

Inside the tent, Lambert stripped to his underwear, lay down on his canvas cot, and pulled the bedsheet up to his chin. His mind-fog had cleared, he was fully conscious now, fully recovered from . . . what? From his own death! There weren't many who could say that. Though he felt very tired, he couldn't sleep, afraid that if he shut his eyes he would die again. But why should he fear it? Dying had been the most wondrous experience of his life. That bliss! Like he'd been injected with some marvelous drug that had taken away all pains, all cares, all desire, all hopes, all dreads, and all awareness of time's arrow, flying relentlessly forward, his grandmother beckoning him to cross the threshold into the mansion of eternity, drenched in unearthly radiance. He yearned to return there and re-experience that perfect joy, even as he clung, with equal force, to the life he knew. Lambert was not religious; yet he was certain he'd been to heaven's gate, until summoned back to the world by . . . *her.* By Marlene, crying out, "He hasn't got a pulse!" then "Wait! I can feel it now. . ."

The wearying struggle to keep his eyes open caused them to shut. He woke two or three hours later, aware that someone was in the tent with him. Rolling onto his side, he blinked against the glare of a headlamp. Delight swept through him when he saw *her*, lying on a cot across from his, her long hair spread across the pillow like a textured shadow. She was reading a paperback.

"Marlene?"

She put the book down. "Ah, you're awake. How are you doing?"

"What are you . . . when did you. . ." he began but couldn't quite form the words.

"About an hour ago. I had my bed moved in here. Someone has to look out for you, just in case, remember? You're okay?"

"I think so. I'm not going to die again. Once is enough."

She laughed the light, chiming laugh that gave him such pleasure. "Sound like your old self. Would you like me to read to you?"

"A bedtime story?"

"Hardly. Jane Austen. Her last novel, *Persuasion.* Maybe not to your taste. *The Short Happy Life of Francis Macomber* would be more in tune with this environment. Will Jane Austen do?"

"Sure," he said, thinking that the sound of her voice would do even if she were reading package directions.

The lamp strapped above her eyes somewhat spoiled the effect of an enchanted princess in her bed; but as she sat up, bowing her head to shine it on the page, he saw that she was wearing a semi-sheer garment, either a cotton shift or a very long T-shirt that reached past her knees and through which the contours of her body showed in the half-light.

"So, *Persuasion* is about a love affair between a woman named Anne Elliot and a Naval officer, Captain Wentworth. They get engaged, but

Anne's family persuade her to break it off because he's not appropriate. They're separated for a long time before they meet again, and . . . well, there's all sorts of complications. They get reacquainted and Wentworth writes a letter to Anne. That's the part I'm on right now."

He motioned to her: go on.

"'I can listen no longer in silence,'" she read with feeling. "'I must speak to you by such means as are within my reach. You pierce my soul. I'm half agony, half hope . . . I offer myself to you again with a heart even more your own, than when you almost broke it eight years and a half ago. . .'"

These words, and the warmth with which Marlene read them, pierced Lambert's soul. They expressed his own emotions, his own thoughts, and overpowered him. He whipped off the bedsheet and threw himself onto his knees beside her and exclaimed that he, too, had to speak by such means as were within his reach, he, too, was half agony, half hope, and offering his heart. Marlene drew back, as if the outburst were a physical assault.

"I'm in love with you, have been for days, only I didn't know it till now."

If he hadn't undergone the experience of a few hours ago, he would have lacked the nerve to make this declaration.

"Go back to bed, Doug," she said, much as a teacher would say, "Go back to your seat" to an unruly student. "Maybe you're not yourself after all."

"I'm very much myself! I want to kiss you and make love to you, here, now. What do you say to that?"

Marlene closed the book, laid it in her lap and said with a cool stare: "Not a thing."

In the morning, he found her sipping coffee at the campfire, smoldering in the cool air. She was alone, and greeted him cheerfully in Swahili,

"*Habari*, Doug. *Habari yako*?" as if nothing had passed between them. He answered that he was fine, all things considered, and dropped into a camp chair. One of Victoria's boys—employees? staff?—brought him a mug of coffee. He hadn't asked for it; his wish had been anticipated and fulfilled. Africa could spoil you if you had status or money, preferably both, and if you were white.

"I got carried away last night," he said, cautiously. "Apologies if I made you uncomfortable."

Actually, he was sorry that he'd embarrassed himself. But at least he'd behaved well, like the gentleman he considered himself to be; after her rebuff, he'd meekly done as she'd asked—gone back to bed.

"You didn't make me uncomfortable at all," she said with a forgiving smile. "Don't give it a second thought."

But he did, and the thought, as he watched sunrise brightening the acacia trees, was that he'd made false assumptions. Her tears when she could not feel his pulse, the rejoicing in her voice when she did, and then moving her bed into his tent had led him to believe that she cared for him, *desired* him, as deeply as he cared for and desired her. Her cutting response, "Not a thing," had proven the fragility of that illusion. Lambert was not accustomed to rejection; the rare instances when a woman turned him down were black swans, if not violations of natural law. He also trusted his instincts, more than he did his powers of reason; and those instincts told him even now that she was attracted to him but was too fixated on her project to express it, or to acknowledge it. Those same instincts likewise told him that she would be, must be, his partner in the Great Romance he'd sought for years. Tracy and Hepburn, Bogie and Bacall—that would be them. The shards of his shattered illusion began to reassemble themselves. His near-death experience had shocked him into the truth of his feelings for Marlene. He could not rely on some similar, random occurrence to awaken her. He would have to do it by nurturing her attraction for him, tending it until she realized she was in love with him.

"We'll be leaving right after breakfast. Pack a toothbrush and a change in case you have to stay the night."

It was Victoria, looking as crisp in her starched khaki jacket as she sounded.

"Leaving?"

"Nairobi. The hospital. Must have you checked out. Two minutes without a heartbeat—nothing to muck about with."

Owing to the condition of the road and to the habits of Kenyan drivers—trailer trucks straddling the centerline so that they couldn't be passed right side or left—the trip took more than six hours. They arrived around three. Lambert had spent some time in various Third World hospitals; he was pleased by the First World sparkle of this one. Victoria went in with him, and was taken for his wife by the nurse at the admissions desk. After setting her straight, she and Lambert waited half an hour in a room with a man trembling and sweating from malaria before they were summoned into the office of Dr. Ronald Andajte, a specialist in tropical diseases. He listened to Victoria's description of Lambert's collapse—the eyes going suddenly blank and still, the cessation of his breathing and pulse—asked Lambert a few questions about his medical history, then scoped his eyes, gave him a blood test and an EKG, and diagnosed "Lariam toxicity." Nothing to be done about it except, one, stop taking the drug; two, no alcohol for at least a week, and three, drink plenty of water to hasten the Lariam, which had a half-life of two to three weeks, out of his system. Any questions?

Lambert thought for a bit before asking Dr. Andajte if he believed that death was the end or a passage to another state of being.

The doctor, a man of around forty-five with a small, aristocratic head and hollow cheekbones, gave him a puzzled look. "That is a question best answered by a minister, not a doctor. Why do you ask?"

Except for the few words he'd spoken to Keyes, Lambert hadn't said a thing about his journey to heaven's gate. Now he did, in detail, and when he finished, he checked Victoria's and the doctor's expressions to see if they thought he'd flipped out. But the doctor only tilted back in his chair and clasped his hands behind his head, a smile blazing across his face.

"Oh, yes. One of those. A near-death experience. They are very much alike—the shimmering light, seeing people long dead, the euphoria," he said in an accent tinged with Oxbridge. Lambert noticed, among the degrees on one wall, that he'd gotten his MD from the Leicester School of Medicine in the UK. "Also, Lariam is known in some cases to have neurological side effects. Hallucinations are not uncommon."

"It was no hallucination. Never had an experience like that. I was perfectly happy. I feel . . . changed."

"Do you mean you were a skeptic, now you're not?"

"I'd say it made me skeptical about my own skepticism."

"I cannot help you in that regard."

"Sometimes I want to go back there and sometimes I'm afraid I will. I had a hard time getting to sleep last night."

"That I can help."

Dr. Andajte whipped out a pen, wrote out a prescription, and said, handing it to Lambert, "There is a chemist in the building. First floor."

Victoria had to stay in Nairobi for a day or two, so she arranged for a small plane to fly Lambert back to Tsavo the next morning. Thanks to Dr. Andajte's pills, he spent a restful night at the Norfolk hotel. He did not die, nor take any mental journeys to the afterworld. Ogeto and Keyes, both wearing clean shirts and clean expedition pants, met him at the airstrip and drove him to camp. Keyes said he was pleased to see Lambert in good health, and glad that he made it back in time for the party.

"It's Marlene's birthday. Thirty-one today. We're celebrating with a picnic. And here she comes, gentlemen."

Lambert almost did not recognize the woman who emerged from her tent, parodying the swagger of an actress at the Academy Awards, the intended comedy undermined by her awareness of the effect her appearance had on her audience. Gone were the baggy safari shorts, the dusty shirt, the scuffed boots, replaced by a blue-and-white dress that clung to her, but not too tightly, and blue pumps; the hair that usually tumbled promiscuously out from under a baseball cap was pinned up in a swirl, its lustrous black accentuating the paleness of her exposed neck.

Keyes borrowed one of Victoria's vehicles—it was in far better condition than his—and drove south for half an hour, then turned onto a little-used two-track and parked on a tabletop ridge, which Ogeto identified as Poachers Lookout. It overlooked the Serengeti, an expanse of grass colored like champagne going on and on into Tanzania and to the foothills of Kilimanjaro. The legendary mountain loomed blue-gray, its middle slopes cloaked by a reef of clouds so that its snowy peak appeared to be levitating nineteen thousand feet above the savannah.

"There it is, looking down on us with all our petty insecurities," Marlene said.

"My insecurities aren't petty," Keyes said.

"And Kili is spiritually dead, like Everest," Lambert added. "Too many people climbing it."

"Ah, the mystic speaks," Marlene teased.

A blanket was spread on the grass, a cooler opened, sandwiches and a chilled white brought forth. While they ate, the biologists spoke of matters biological, criticizing a colleague named June for her tendency to anthropomorphize animals. Sure, they were smarter than people gave them credit for, said Keyes, but the brightest Bonobo, the Einstein of Bonobos, would never be able to add two and two. Marlene turned to Lambert, a teasing sparkle in her eyes.

"You agree?"

He nodded vaguely, captivated by the sight she made as she sat in her incongruous garden-party dress, its hem riding up past her knees.

"I know you think that we scientists want to demystify nature, but you're wrong. We just want to clarify what the *real* mysteries are."

"Let me take your photo," he said.

Keyes and Ogeto obligingly moved out of the shot as Marlene struck a Wind-in-the-Willows pose, leaning back to rest on her hands, her head tilted ever so slightly to one side. Lambert zoomed in, zoomed out, making love to her with his film camera, a Leica.

"How about one of you and me together?" she said after he'd exposed five or six frames. He was stunned, and thrilled as he passed the camera to Keyes. Marlene stood, smoothing her dress with her palms. Lambert placed an arm around her waist, waited to feel her stiffen, and was more deeply thrilled when instead she slouched into him and hugged his waist.

"Smile," Keyes said.

Standing next to her, her arm pressed tight against his back, Lambert was sure that if he did not convince her to love him—no, to confess that she already did love him—he would fall down and die again. In one of their quarrels, Letitia, his last wife, had asked him, "How is it that someone who sees the real world through a viewfinder can't see things as they are with the eyes in his head?" Lambert's imagination was the answer. It was too powerful, and it seized him now and flew away with him. Marlene and he would travel the world together, she joining him on assignments, he accompanying her on expeditions. They would eat roast goat over Mongolian fires and have wild sex in yurts; they would dine at the Antico Arco in Rome and muss the bedsheets in the Paris Ritz. Tracy and Hepburn, Bogey and Bacall, the envy of other couples, manacled to their mortgaged lives.

Victoria returned the following afternoon with news she'd picked up at park HQ from Beech: he'd located a black-maned lion and had photographed it.

"Quite surprised he spoke to me, bygones be bygones. I asked him to email the picture," she said, tapping her cellphone screen.

She passed the phone around the dining table, littered with lunch dishes waiting to be cleared and washed. Lambert, Marlene, Keyes, and Ogeto got a look at a great brute of a lion, long-legged, well-muscled, probably over four hundred pounds, with a sparse mane nearly as charcoal-hued as Marlene's hair. Beech had captured him broadside—it was as though he were posing—on a vast sun-blasted plain, thornbush thickets in the near background, broken hills far off. Hindquarters of two more lions could be seen at the left edge of the picture.

"A bachelor group," Victoria said. "Sticking together till they're ready to establish prides of their own."

"The others are blond?" asked Marlene. "I'll need a blond for the dominance comparison."

"Probably, I can't say for sure, but there is this problem. . ."

Marlene's breath caught. "Problem? There's no problem. It's a perfect setup! Couldn't have ordered a better one myself!"

Victoria raised a finger to say "Wait," then went out to her car. She came back with a map under her arm, unrolled it on the table, and pinned the corners with coffee cups.

"The problem is that your dark-haired boy is here." With a pencil, she drew a small circle in a region north of the Galana River. "This entire area is off-limits to visitors. It's dangerous. A hunting ground for ivory poachers."

Her stare roamed over their faces.

"It is, yes, so what was Mister Beech doing there?" Ogeto said, his forehead wrinkling.

"I assume that when the director gave him run of the park, he meant all of it. But you people would need a special permit. I've already put a request in. Talked you up—you're not visitors, not tourists . . . engaged in serious scientific work. The director has to get the okay from Nairobi to issue it. He wasn't optimistic, but should you get it, he'll assign a couple of KWS rangers for security."

Marlene asked how long before they heard from the director. Victoria shrugged. Could be this afternoon, or tomorrow, or never.

Keyes blew through his nostrils. "We've already extended our stay here by ten days, and only three of those are left. Two, really—today's shot. If we left now, the lions would be laid up by the time we got out there."

"Nothing for it now but to wait. I'll let you know when and if I hear anything."

Victoria turned and left. Marlene settled slowly into a chair, her shoulders slumped, her hands dangling between her knees.

"I don't believe years of work, I don't believe that my doctorate now hinges on the whim of some bureaucrat in Nairobi. Ogeto . . . have you ever been out that way?"

"Twice, with anti-poaching squads."

"Is it all that dangerous?"

"That depends."

"On what?"

"On what—who—you run into. Somali *shifti,* with their AK-47s, very dangerous. If only local poachers, not so much. Waliangulu, most of them, The People of the Long Bow. Of course, you may not run into anyone, and in that case, no danger at all."

"These Wali-whatchyacallem. . ."

"Waliangulu. They have been hunting elephants for a thousand years. They are the ones who killed Satao, a big, oh, a very big tusker not long ago. Each one forty kilos. They hunt them now for profit. With their bows and arrows. Those do not make noise like an AK."

"Bow and arrows? Elephants?" Marlene said.

"Yes. The arrows are poisoned. I don't know if it has a name. It is brewed from the fruit of the *Akokanthera* shrub. The Waliangulu dip the arrowheads in it. Most toxic. It can kill five or six tons of elephant in hours, much less time to kill a man. Minutes sometimes."

"But these people aren't as dangerous as the *shifti*?"

"Is a bow as dangerous as an assault rifle?"

Marlene straightened her posture. Her thoughts were an easy read, and Keyes, with a sharp look, shaking his head, told her to stop thinking them.

"Like the lady said, nothing to do but wait," he said. "And if we don't get the permit, don't worry. You have enough observations as it is. You'll be Dr. Ryder soon enough. Guaranteed."

"I'll hold you to that," she said, bestowing a smile on her faculty advisor. "I'll get Lothario and Fabrizio coiffed and the sound equipment ready to go. Just in case we get our permission slip."

"I'd like to see them," Lambert said.

He followed her to the tent where she and Keyes stored their gear: night-vision goggles, thermal imaging camera, tape recorders and tapes of various roars, grunts, and cackles, and the two dummy lions. They stood in the rear, life-size impersonations with glass eyes, stuffed bodies covered in tan fabric. Four imitation manes hung from the ridgepole, like wigs in an actor's dressing room: long and short blondes, long and short dark ones.

"A taxidermist made these for us," Marlene said. "They look real enough to fool a lion until he gives them the sniff test. It's why we're here—we used up every lion in our study area in the Serengeti. They were on to the trick."

Lambert attached a flash to his digital Canon and photographed Marlene placing the short blonde mane on the head of one dummy—Fabrizio—and the short dark mane on the other—Lothario. She combed them with her fingers and stepped back.

"So, what do you think?"

"They could fool me," he said. "If I stumbled in here and saw them in this dim light I'd piss my pants."

"You don't strike me as the pants-wetter type."

"I'm flattered you think so."

"Keyes lent me a book you're mentioned in. It's mostly about Peter Beard, but you are mentioned—flatteringly—in a few places."

"Peter Beard was a great photographer until he became a celebrity. Took up with society women and models, hung out with Andy Warhol and that crew. Blew his talent on being famous and good looking. He was one handsome son of a bitch, still is, even at eighty. I'll say that for him."

"You knew him?"

"Casually. You could say, now, that he and I have one thing in common besides photographing wildlife, and I don't mean our looks."

"I read about that. He was gored by an elephant about twenty years ago. No pulse when his friends got him to a hospital. Clinically dead and then he came back to life. You, Peter Beard, and Jesus, the three resurrectos." The windchimes rang again in her laughter. She smoothed Lothario's mane with her palm and blinked as the flash fired. "You're not so bad looking yourself, y'know."

"Flattered again," he said, his scalp and forearms tingling.

He took the compliment as an invitation, looped his arms around her waist, drew her to him, and kissed her, his tongue licking the inside of her lips. She did not return the kiss, nor did she resist, merely stood limp in his embrace before pulling her mouth from his.

"You didn't ask permission this time," she said.

"I didn't last time either. It was more a proposal. But feel free to sue me for sexual harassment."

"I'll make it sexual assault. I don't believe in half measures," she giggled, and gave him a gentle shove backwards.

Lambert almost wished his kiss had offended her; any reaction would have been preferable to her flip indifference.

Returning her attention to the dummies, she resumed coiffing their manes. "You boys are key to me getting somewhere. One more data point, that's all I need."

"Keyes told you that you'll get your doctorate with or without that . . . that data point."

"Oh, it's a question of doing something exceptional, something no one's done before. That's cited in professional journals."

"In other words, you don't want to be Dr. Marlene Ryder. You want to be *the* Dr. Marlene Ryder."

She stopped the obsessive grooming, and crossing her hands, rested them on Lothario's neck.

"Frankly, yes. There's nothing wrong with ambition."

Lambert agreed. He understood ambition, the greed for recognition. Although being known as the person who'd determined why lions sported manes still seemed to him a less than headline-grabbing discovery.

"Means a lot to you?"

"That oughtta be clear by now."

"Wait here," he said.

Going to the dining hall, he saw that Victoria had left the map on the table. Good. Saved him a step. He took his GPS from his pocket, plugged in the coordinates of the penciled circle marking where Beech had sighted the black-maned lion, then toggled the buttons on the instrument. A red line appeared on the screen, showing him the direction from camp, and a number on a bar at the top gave him the straight-line distance. Of course that didn't tell him how far it was by road, so he tore a sheet from his notebook, laid it on the map's distance scale, and penciled a line on the note paper. From one edge of the page to that line represented five miles. This crude ruler he placed on the roads leading to the lion's location, ticking off each segment with his pencil. That done, he returned to Marlene with the map, which he spread on the tent floor.

"It's forty miles by road, give or take, to here," he said, placing his finger on the circle. "Maybe a ninety-minute drive if we don't have any more battery problems."

Marlene paused for a long moment. She swallowed. "What exactly are you. . ."

"I think you know what. It's your idea. Been in your head since Victoria showed us the picture. I'm just giving it some shape, showing you how to carry it out. How long will it take to run your whatever it is . . . experiment?"

"An hour, maybe two."

"Let's say two. If we leave at four tomorrow, we could be back here before lunch. All goes well, you'll have this data point you're after. I'll take photos to prove it."

"And Keyes?"

"I'll leave him a note that we've gone on a scout, like we've done every morning, only we left a little earlier than usual. I won't tell him where."

Her fingers nervously plucked the dummy's skin, as if she were pulling off ticks. But the very risks that made her apprehensive also excited her; Lambert saw the excitement flickering in her luminous eyes.

"What if that lion Beech photographed is nowhere near where he said it was?" she said. "That guy has every reason to be pissed off at us. It would be just like him to send us off on a wild goose chase. Or a way to stick his thumb in our eyes—I know where you can find what you're looking for, but you can't go there, you'll need me."

"Yeah, I had the same thought. I don't see any other way but to give it a try."

"Why are you doing this?" she asked.

"I think you know that, too."

With Marlene at the wheel and Lambert in the passenger seat, the dash-mounted GPS switched on, his own instrument and the map on his lap, they left camp at precisely six minutes past four, towing Lothario and Fabrizio in a horse trailer. They drove for about an hour, headlights turning the red roads to white, the sky paling to extinguish the stars of the southern hemisphere. A concrete bridge conveyed them across the Galana, slick and shallow and gray in the semi-darkness. Five more miles brought them to a fork. Lambert glanced at the map and directed Marlene to take the road on the right. The sun cracked over the horizon, its light washing over an immense plain, like a waterless sea islanded by thornbush thickets and clumps of acacia. A termite mound ten or twelve feet high, castellated with turrets and towers, rose near the roadside, and farther off, a Cape buffalo herd showed as a single black, shiny mass, slowly moving. Sacred ibis waded in a waterhole.

"*Threskiornis aethiopicus*," Lambert said, showing off his wildlife erudition. "Symbol of the Egyptian god Thoth, god of the moon and of learning."

"Thank you, Mister Wizard," quipped Marlene. "How much farther?"

"Another fifteen or twenty minutes should put us there."

"The chances that they'll be right where Beech spotted them are nil. Bachelor groups move around quite a lot, looking for the same thing as human bachelors."

"But they should be in the general area."

"Yup. I'll call them in with a recording. A lioness in heat."

This is how it would be, Lambert thought, looking at the straight, coral-colored road spooling out across the plain ahead. The two of us bantering as we set off into the wild unknown. Maybe we would do a book together. A classy coffee table book, text by Marlene Ryder, photos by Douglas Lambert. A launch party in Manhattan, Marlene ravishing in a low-cut cocktail dress, me pulling it off in the hotel room afterward.

His GPS beeped. A message—ARRIVED WAYPOINT 256—flashed onscreen. The GPS on the dash confirmed. To the right, two or three hundred yards away, a meandering line of thornbush marked the course of a lugga.

"Any money they're hunkered down somewhere in there," Marlee said as she pulled off the road a short distance, finding some concealment for the vehicle under a majestic baobab.

The dry-season wind had not yet begun to blow, the morning air was perfectly still, so they needn't worry that the lions—if they were near—would catch their scent. They hauled the dummies out of the trailer to an open spot a safe distance away. Marlene placed them side by side, several yards apart; then, returning to the Land Rover, she hooked up the sound equipment. Lambert climbed into a rear seat, lowered the window part-way, and braced his camera on it. The digital—he wasn't concerned with making art, this would be for purposes of documentation. He shot a few frames through a 200-millimeter lens and looked at the LCD screen to check if the shutter speed, aperture, and focus settings were spot on. They were.

Binoculars strung from her neck, Marlene stood on the front seat, her head and shoulders poking through the roof hatch.

"Ready?" she asked in an undertone.

Lambert gave her a thumbs up. She aimed the speaker at the thorn-bush galleried along the lugga, powered on the amplifier, and played the grunts and roars of a lioness lusting to mate.

"That should get the attention of any red-blooded male in the vicinity," she said.

She scanned right to left, left to right with binoculars, but saw nothing. After waiting five minutes, she cranked up the amp. Still no sign of anything. She rapped the roof with a fist and silenced the recording. "Damn! Damn!"

Not ten seconds later, Lambert spotted them. "Look left. Three, four hundred yards," he said in a near whisper.

She swiveled the binoculars, and in a strangled voice, croaked, "Oh my God! It's them! Two blondes and a black, and the black is leading the way!"

She bounced up and down, like an excited kid, as the trio approached, hugging the thornbush. They had not yet spotted the dummies. Marlene turned the recorder back on and the grunts and roars sounded again. The three lions stopped for a second, then recommenced their advance. When they were about two hundred yards away, they caught sight of Lothario and Fabrizio. They turned and began to move toward the dummies, very cautiously, the two blondes behind and slightly to one side of the dark-maned male. Lambert zeroed his camera on their faces, which showed both wariness and deliberation. Their movements were choreographed

—black mane would creep forward and halt, the blondes would come up; then he would creep forward again. To Lambert, they looked like infantrymen covering each other as they advanced in enemy territory. His motor drive whirred. The move-pause-move sequence continued until the dark male was within twenty yards of Fabrizio, the light-haired dummy. He became a blur as he charged, and letting out a fearsome roar, smacked Fabrizio with a forepaw, knocking the dummy over. He backed off, confused because he'd expected a fight. He sniffed beneath Fabrizio's tail, joined in a moment by his two fair buddies. Realizing they'd been duped, they all three trotted off. Marlene, pressing the Land Rover's horn with her foot, startled them into a run.

"My God, oh, my God!" she cried out. "Do you know how long it's taken me to get to this point? Dark manes are a turn-on for females, they intimidate males."

They retrieved the dummies, shoved them back into the horse trailer. Fabrizio's face had been ripped open by his attacker, stuffing bulged through the tears instead of muscle and bone.

"You got pictures?" she asked.

"More than enough," he said, and showed her a few on the LCD viewer.

"All right! Proof positive! Now . . . now you can kiss me."

With his heart thumping against his ribs, he did, and this time she returned the kiss, though she did so more in gratitude or perhaps to celebrate her triumph.

"We make a good team, don't you think? After you get your PhD, maybe we could, y'know. . ."

She responded to the half-spoken overture with an enigmatic tilt of her lovely head; but he was not discouraged.

On the return drive, Marlene, her mission accomplished, was as relaxed and happy as Lambert had seen her in the past three weeks. She stopped once to study a large bird perched in a tree—an African Crowned Eagle—another time to admire a rare oryx, a fine specimen with its slender, half-black, half-white legs, its long, backswept horns glinting in the harsh sunlight. First one she'd seen in the wild, even though she'd been a year in Africa. They both gasped as they approached the waterhole where they'd seen the sacred Ibis. In it, an elephant stood drinking; a bull that looked like an enormous terra cotta statue, hide red with Tsavo dust and dried mud. Its tusks, curving inward, almost touched the ground.

"They must go a hundred plus each," Lambert said. "Stop. I've got to get shots of him."

He opened the door carefully and crouched behind the Land Rover, spreading his elbows on the hood to form a bipod for his camera. Facing the road, the great bull with tusks like gigantic scimitars filled the view-finder. Lambert could see its huge, brown, intelligent eyes as it lowered its trunk into the water, raised and bent it into his mouth. He could likewise see the bull double-paged in *Geographic* or on the covers of guidebooks, and the credit line beneath: PHOTO BY DOUGLAS LAMBERT.

The elephant drank deeply; it probably had trudged miles to find water in the dry season, and there wasn't a lot of it in the waterhole. When it had its fill, it turned, stirring muck from the bottom, and plodded out of the waterhole toward a tree line in the near distance. Then it stopped, swaying back and forth before it collapsed to all four knees all at once, its six tons crashing to the ground with such force Lambert heard the thud from a hundred yards away. Moments later, it rolled over onto its side, its hind legs thrashing; then it lay as motionless as a boulder.

Lambert and Marlene stared, unable to process what they had just seen. There had been no gunshot; nor, recalling what Ogeto had said about the Waliangulu, did he see an arrow shaft protruding from the body. Anyway, no arrow on earth or elsewhere could drop such a bull elephant so suddenly.

"Doug! He's dead!" Marlene had the binoculars trained on the beast. "I don't see that he's breathing."

"Elephants don't just drop dead for no reason. I'm going to have a look," he said. "Stay here."

"No way I will."

He knew she would say that. They scared a covey of sandgrouse into flight as they skirted the waterhole, approaching the elephant from behind. When within fifty feet, Lambert pitched stones at its backside to make sure it was dead. The bull lay still, immense and tragic. Marlene and Lambert both felt that something grand had passed out of the world. They walked around the carcass, gazed, marveling at the tusks, each six feet in length and as thick at the base as a small tree.

"I said a hundred, more like a hundred fifteen," Lambert said. "There aren't twenty bulls in all of Africa with tusks that size."

They passed around the gigantic head, and spotted an abscess in the elephant's side, behind its rib cage. The grapefruit-size bulge was covered in flies and oozed pus and a ribbon of some black liquid, like tar only thinner.

"That's what did it?" Lambert said, thinking aloud. "Injured in a fight with another bull?"

Marlene stepped closer and craned her neck forward, squinting at the wound. Then she jumped back, as though something had lunged at her from out of the festering wound. "Let's get out of here, Doug."

"What's the matter?"

"There's a broken shaft in there, and my guess is with an arrowhead at the end of it. Poachers. Poachers did that. The poor animal has probably been walking around for hours with that in him."

Lambert bent toward the abscess and saw the broken shaft inside. It must have cracked in two when the huge bull, running after it was hit, bumped against a tree trunk. A magnificent creature slaughtered so someone somewhere could wear an ivory bracelet, so someone somewhere else could display an ivory trinket on a mantlepiece. He decided to document this murder. What other word could there be for it? Because his bag with short focal length lenses was in the Land Rover, he moved back several yards to better focus the 200-millimeter. He framed the festering abscess and took half a dozen shots. A police photographer at a crime scene.

"We're going to show these to KWS, get them to bust whoever did this," he said, partly from outrage, partly because he thought Marlene would appreciate his zeal for animal justice. "Better yet"—pulling his cellphone from his back pocket—"I'm going to call them right now to send a team out here."

"Getting out of here is what we're going to do right now," she snapped, sounding like an irritated wife. "There's no cell service out here anyway. You can call from camp."

She turned and walked quickly toward the car, Lambert following with the phone in his ear, on the chance that he would pick up a signal. He understood the reason for her urgency: the elephant was carrying a fortune in ivory; the poachers, tracking it, waiting for it die, might be nearby.

Marlene jumped into the Land Rover, as agilely as she had when they'd pushed it down into the drift. Reaching over the front seat, she swung the passenger door open for him. He was half inside when he felt something slice his right shoulder, a quick, sharp sensation, like he'd been slashed with a straight razor.

Waliangulu longbows are thought to be as powerful as the armor-piercing weapons wielded by the English archers at Agincourt; they must be to penetrate an elephant's thick hide. The missile that had grazed Lambert's shoulder shot right through the door window, shattering it, then tumbled to the ground. He threw himself into the seat, Marlene floored the pedal, the sudden acceleration swinging the door shut, and sped off, the vehicle pluming reddish dust. Lambert clutched his shoulder with his free hand and looked with a mixture of horror and morbid fascination at the blood streaming through his fingers. He squeezed them to stop the flow and felt an indentation in his triceps; the arrow had clipped a part of it off. After they'd gone banging over dips and ruts at fifty miles an hour, he asked Marlene to ease up on the gas; his whole upper arm was throbbing, and every jolt sent electric shock through it.

"Have you got a first aid kit in here?"

She shook her head, then slowed down, stopped, and pulled a bundle of rags from out of the glove compartment. Leaning over him so he could feel the warmth of her cheek, she yanked at his ripped sleeve, tore it off, and looped one rag under his injured arm and cinched it as a tourniquet. Another she pressed to the wound, gaping like a bloodied mouth, and tied it with a third. Her competence, her lack of squeamishness as she wiped her hands clean, moved him.

They drove on, again at breakneck speed. "Got to get you back as fast as we can. Victoria will radio the Flying Doctor Service."

"A half second earlier, that arrow would hit me square in the back," he said, thinking how absurd it is to be shot with an arrow in the twenty-first century.

"But it didn't," she said. "Beech. He's had it in for us. Now I think we know why he told Victoria where the lion was."

He grasped what she was driving at and said that it was far-fetched. He noticed that his jaw stiffened as he spoke. Tetanus? No. Tetanus took a long time to set in.

"Maybe," she said. "But I'll bet he's in with the poachers, probably scouts for them, gets a cut of the money. He gave them a heads up to be on the lookout for us."

"But how. . ." Lambert twitched his jaw back and forth, trying to work the tightness out of it. "How could he have known we'd take the . . . the bait."

"We'll deal with that later, after we get you to Nairobi."

They rattled over the Galana bridge. A little way upstream, a zebra herd stood near the bank, a single mass of black and white stripes, each animal motionless as the stallions eyed the river for crocodiles before giving the signal that it was safe to drink. Lambert sensed their desperate thirst, shared in it, for his own mouth felt stuffed with cotton wool. He reached for a water bottle wedged under his seat, but he could barely move his good arm. Finally, he managed to grab the bottle, tipped it to his lips, forced his mouth to open, and sucked like a baby on a tit. Most of the water dribbled down his chin. He moaned.

"Doug? Are you all right?"

"Something sitting on me . . . heavy. . ."

"Hang in there. You hang in there, we'll be home soon."

Then he saw who, or what, was on his lap, crushing his legs, embracing him with its arms, squeezing his chest so that every breath was an effort. The black-winged angel. Panic rushed into him and through him, his heart palpitating. Was he dying? From a non-fatal wound? Didn't make sense. From what, then? He gasped when a convulsion slammed his head against the back of the seat so that he was looking straight up through the roof hatch, a bright rectangle.

"Hang on! Hang in there!"

Marlene sounded far away. She sped over the rutted road and hit a bump that bounced Lambert six inches off the seat and flung the angel right through the hatch. He followed its flight into the sky. Relieved of its weight, he imagined that he was soaring with it, though he did not lose sight of the bright rectangle. His heart rate slowed, skipped a beat, slowed a little more. He knew then that the question he'd asked the doctor in Nairobi would soon be answered. Nothing else mattered. Winning Marlene's love did not matter. The foolish desire of a foolish, aging man. He did not see the glorious light, nor the mansion crowded with dead friends and relatives, nor his grandmother, only the blue patch in the roof, its corners rounding off into a circle that grew ever smaller, like a camera's shutter closing in slow motion.

All four of them, Marlene—Keyes, Ogeto, and Victoria—stood at the airstrip and watched the Cessna carrying Lambert's body climb, then turn northward. The American embassy in Nairobi would be responsible for transferring him to next of kin. They kept their eyes on the plane until it vanished from sight, then started back toward the cluster of green tents.

Marlene, with Lambert's camera slung over her shoulder, kicked at the dirt as she walked.

"What did you say that poison is called?" she asked Ogeto.

Ogeto stopped in his tracks, and clasped her arm, stopping her. "And would the name have made any difference?"

"Yeah, would *that* have stopped you two from doing what you did?" said Keyes, bitterness in his voice.

"It was Doug's idea. I just . . . I went along with it. . . . Oh, Keyes, I never would have. . ."

She stifled a sob and trailed off.

"You should have told him no. He was ga-ga over you. Plain to see. Do you really think you're worth dying for?"

"That's low, Keyes. That's very, very low."

"No squabbles, please," Victoria cut in. She pointed ahead at a KWS vehicle parked in camp. "You're going to have to give them a statement. Remember, your GPS went on the fritz, you took a wrong turn, got lost."

"It'll be the first time I ever lied to a cop."

"First time for everything. They'll want to keep a lid on this. A photographer murdered in the park—awfully bad for tourism."

A pack of hyenas, hidden in the long grass beyond camp, whooped and cackled. It sounded like a madman's laughter.

THE DELIVERER

It was more roar than howl, a deep-in-the-throat bellowing in the forest at the river's edge, and it seemed to make the air vibrate. Covington flinched, tightened his grip on the panga's gunwales, as if he were in a storm and afraid of being thrown overboard.

"Stand easy," said Tyner from the thwart in the stern. "Only a Howler Monkey."

Covington had spent much of his career pilfering ruins in Mexico. This was his first venture into Central America.

"I know what it is." He spoke with a cultivated accent that sounded vaguely British. "Wasn't expecting it. They usually let loose at dawn."

"Dusk, too," Tyner said.

"Well, it's. . ." Covington looked at his watch. "A little past two in the afternoon."

"Maybe this monkey slept in and is just waking up."

From the bow, Isaac thrust out one scrawny brown arm, signaling Tyner to turn into a tributary. The rainy season had come and the tributary, like the main stem, was mud-colored and swollen. The spaces between the dense trees on both sides looked like dark cracks in green walls. Thin branches bowed low; their tips scratched riffles in the current.

Tyner had throttled down almost to an idle; without the breeze the faster passage on the river had afforded, he was soon dripping sweat as bounteous as the raindrops falling from the leaves. The tributary was shallowing, the bottom was visible now. He tilted the engine to avoid striking the prop on a rock or sunken log.

He slapped a mosquito on his cheek and said, "Yo, Isaac. Skinny water getting skinnier. How much farther?"

Isaac made a half turn of his head to look at Tyner over his shoulder. "Not far," he said.

"How far is not far, goddamnit."

"Ain't too far at all."

"Fucking savage," Tyner said under his breath; but less than ten minutes later, with barely more than a foot under the keel, Isaac pointed to where a swath of slick mud, like a gator's belly drag, slid from the jungle into the water.

"Put her in there," he said.

After Tyner had done this and secured the panga's bowline to a tree, he and Covington sprayed their hands with repellant and rubbed it into their faces and necks. Tyner hoisted a small pack containing two plastic water bottles and a 40-caliber pistol with three snake loads and four 180-grain cartridges in the magazine. Covington shouldered a bigger pack loaded with a small shovel and brushes and archeological trowels. Isaac had told him he wouldn't need the tools, but he'd brought them anyway.

Isaac led off down a path, which was sufficiently traveled that he did not need the machete belted to his waist to clear brush or vines.

"So, Isaac, if I was to ask how far to the ruins, would you tell us that it isn't far?" Covington asked, trying to sound jovial and relaxed.

"Exactly what I gon ta tell you, cuz that's how far it is."

"You and your partner, you're sure you're the only ones who've been in here? This trail looks like it's been used a lot."

"It's me my partner been usin' it."

Roots thick as lampposts and slender as wands writhed across the path, which twisted under mahogany and ceiba and fan palms and the zapote Isaac had harvested before he and another chiclero discovered the ruins. The discovery had been accidental; they'd stumbled upon them while seeking new trees to tap. The artifacts they'd found were plentiful and valuable enough to afford them a living far better than they could earn extracting the reddish sap from which chewing gum was made.

Cicadas were singing, their collective whine deafening at times. "Okay, we here!" Isaac shouted over the noise as they came into a clearing where mounds covered in vines and ferns rose like enormous, green anthills. Four of them were arranged to form a square. Isaac, whacking at the vines with the machete, went around to the back side of the nearest mound. A flock of parrots shrieked, and when they and the cicada ceased their racket, the silence was so deep as to be a sound in itself. It was broken by a rustling in the underbrush, a loud rustling.

"What's that?" asked Covington. He was still trying to sound relaxed, but this attempt was less successful.

Isaac and Tyner listened and Tyner said, "It's nothing."

"It sounded big."

"Jaguar, mebbe," said Isaac. "Maya people, they believe them jaguar guards this place."

"A jaguar isn't nothing."

"Dude, seems like every little noise gets you ready to jump out of your skin," Tyner said. "Need a tranquilizer?"

"Your job was to get us in here by boat and then get us out. That's all. So stay in your lane."

Isaac sheathed the machete and stepped into a shallow ditch that led into a looters' trench bored into the heart of the mound like a mineshaft. A stele at the entrance had hieroglyphics and mysterious figures chiseled into it. "Classical period," said Covington. "See this,"—he pointed at glyphs beneath the carving of a thing that looked half-human, half-beast—"the sculptor's signature and the date: October 15, 750 AD on our calendar."

"C'mon. You can read that?" Tyner asked skeptically.

"I just did."

Covington and Isaac strapped on headlamps, then entered the tunnel,

Isaac again in the lead. The air inside was thick and smelled of rot, it smelled as if neither wind nor breeze had disturbed it in a thousand years. The headlamp beams played along bare limestone blocks lining both sides. A few yards ahead, the tunnel came to an end in a wall of blocks cut in perfect rectangles, also bare except for one, about five feet above the bottom, bearing more glyphic inscriptions.

"I suppose you can read that, too," Tyner said in a low voice.

Covington squinted. "It's an epitaph for a high priest. My guess is that there's a funeral chamber on the other side of that wall. He died in 785. March 5th, 785 to be exact."

"You've got to be full of. . ."

Isaac let out a sharp yip and jumped backwards, bumping into Covington. "Tommygoff! Shit!"

Twenty-eight years at sea—four in the US Navy, two crewing on commercial fishing boats, three more on ocean racers, and the last nineteen as a delivery captain ferrying yachts to their millionaire and billionaire owners across half the world—had sharpened the division between the hemispheres in Kirby's brain to the point that they had very little to say to each other. The left side was firmly moored to the stern practicalities needed to keep a vessel afloat and on course, while the right was marinated in nautical superstitions—bananas on board bring bad luck, never rename a boat without first conducting a de-naming ceremony—to cite just two of a thousand myths seamen have sworn by since Roman galleys were the slickest thing on the water. In spite of their near total absence of communication, Kirby's right and left brains coexisted peaceably. They seldom interfered with each other: the right's mystical beliefs did not dominate Kirby's thoughts when, say, he had some navigational problem to solve; nor did the left dismiss its opposite as a trash bin of silly folklore.

This mental split had some bearing on what happened on the delivery of the *Cuyahoga,* a sixty-year-old, once-elegant, much-abused ketch. She was a boat that aspired to the status of a small ship: seventy-two feet at the waterline, eighty overall, with a sail area sufficient to blanket a fair-sized lawn. Her former owner, a drug smuggler, hadn't taken good care of her, and after his arrest and incarceration, she'd deteriorated further in drydock. Boats, like sailors, generally go to hell on land.

She is back in the water now, tied up to a wharf on Ambergris Caye. Kirby has contracted to sail her across two thousand miles of open ocean to Bermuda, where her new owner, a hedge-fund manager named Heineman, plans to haul her out for a top-to-bottom, stem-to-stern restoration to her former glory. Until yesterday, her crew consisted of, besides Kirby, two friends who'd sailed with him on previous deliveries: Mike Ahern, his first mate, and John D'Souza, a boatyard manager who was a decent shipboard cook and a better diesel mechanic.

Just twenty-four hours before *Cuyahoga's* scheduled departure, D'Souza rented a motorbike, intending to tour the Caye. Partway through this excursion, he flipped the bike on a stretch of muddy road, suffering a concussion and a compound fracture of his left leg. Getting him to a hospital on the mainland, then onto a flight back to the States, consumed two full days and demanded full use of Kirby's left-brain faculties; if it hadn't, the right might have taken over and regarded D'Souza's loss as a bad omen.

Tired and frazzled, he returned to Ambergris early the next morning, figuring that he and Ahern were capable of sailing *Cuyahoga* on their own, despite her condition. Still, he spread the word all along the waterfront that he was looking for another crewman.

"So how is our Portuguese man o' war?" Ahern asks when Kirby is again on board.

"He'll live to screw up another day. I'll miss his cooking. The man can broil."

"And we'll miss him even more if we get serious engine trouble," Ahern says in a rumbling voice that sounds as if his vocal cords are in his chest. He looks like a superannuated hippie crossbred to a biker: gray ponytail, scruffy gray beard, pro wrestler's arms lavishly tattooed. "The Perkins in this old girl belongs in a museum, and I doubt the electrical in her has been overhauled since her last rehab back in the whenever."

"Heineman told me it was in ninety-two," Kirby replies.

"Twenty-five years. I'd feel a lot better with John on board."

"Makes two of us. But we'll get the old girl to Bermuda." Kirby fetches a beer from the ice chest wedged into a corner of the cockpit's seats. Much of the ice has melted and the bottle is almost as wet on the outside as on the inside. He lays a damp palm on his partner's knee. "Hell, Mike, you and me, we've delivered from Miami to the Med, Antilles to the Azores."

"Yeah, in boats that were in Bristol shape. Did you contact Heinemann that we'll be late?"

Kirby nods. "He understands that boats don't have ETAs, only destinations. I'm going to take another look around, then we'll shove off."

Leaving his beer half full, he paces the ketch's sun-bleached teak deck, checking fittings, checking stays for tautness, looking for signs of dry rot, and in general trying to get a feel for her. Unlike powerboats, those fiberglass atrocities manufactured for weekend yachtsmen, sailing vessels are living beings, each with its own personality. Kirby knows his own, a thirty-two-foot sloop moored in Newport harbor, as well as a long-married man knows his spouse; but the boats he commands on deliveries are strangers. It is essential to establish a rapport with each one, to learn her capacities, her quirks, her temperament, as quickly as possible. He would not be on intimate terms with *Cuyahoga* until she'd been underway for a day or two; but the process of acquaintanceship must begin before she's at sea.

The morning is fine and clear, still cool, though it bears hints of the cloying heat that will descend soon enough. After inspecting the anchor rode for frays—there were a few—he stands and stretches and watches two gaff-rigged lighters sail into the harbor. A lovely sight, sails bellied in a brisk southwester. Someone on the wharf behind him says: "They're bringing in mainland sand for a construction project. Beach sand on the island is too salty for that."

Turning, he sees a tall young man, slender bordering on skinny, with a hayrick of curly blond hair. He's dressed in a beach bum's outfit—knee-length shorts in rainbow colors, a T-shirt touting a local bar in faded letters, a pair of worn deck shoes.

"They sure are pretty," he says, indicating the lighters. "Hey, could I talk to the skipper?"

"You are," Kirby says.

"You're him?"

"Yup. What do you want?"

The kid (as Kirby sees him, though he looks to be in his mid-to-late twenties), rocks slightly side to side, his lips forming a smile part-hopeful, part bashful.

"I heard that you lost a crewman."

"Who are you and where'd you hear that?"

"Jed Tyner. Some people were talking in this bar." He points at the one advertised on his T-shirt. "Might've been just scuttlebutt, but thought I'd check it out."

"So, you're here for a job interview?"

"Not a job you get paid for. See, it's like this . . . I'm flat broke and I need to get home. To the States."

"Know anything about sailboats? That's key."

"Dude! I sure do. I've crewed on. . ."

"Listen, unless and until we get to know each other better, it's skipper, or captain, or sir. Save 'dude' for your friends."

Tyner's face, already red from sunburn, reddens further. "Hey, forgot my manners. 'Dude' is, like, a habit."

The apology, and Tyner's embarrassment, softens Kirby somewhat. To test his knowledge, he asks him to describe what type of boat the *Cuyahoga* is. Tyner answers: "A ketch, clipper-bowed. She could be a sister to the *Ticonderoga*."

"You know the *Ti*?"

"Yes, sir. Crewed on her a couple of years back."

Impressive, if true. Kirby expands his examination, asking the difference between close hauled and close reach, broad reach and run, and other elementary questions. Tyner answers all confidently and correctly. Kirby steps off the boat onto the dock and softens a little more because looking at Tyner close up is like looking into a mirror that is also a time machine: He'd had curly blond hair when he had more hair, and had been underweight for his height, and the younger man's ears are small, his eyes dark blue, much like Kirby's. Circumstances are also the same, or almost the same; he'd begged his way onto his first voyage under sail when he was young, although, fresh out of the Navy, he hadn't been broke.

"Where're you trying to get to, Tyner?"

"Florida. Jacksonville. I'm from J-ville, but anywhere on the East or Gulf Coast will do."

"We're not headed for the States. Bermuda."

The hopeful look on Tyner's boyish face fades somewhat. He lowers his glance to his shoes. A big toe peeks from a rip in the stitching.

"Wouldn't it be easier if you just flew home from here?"

"Wanna buy me a ticket? I'm broke, like I said. River robbers. You've heard about them?"

Kirby answers that he has not.

"There's these gangs on the mainland. They move up and down the river at night in dugouts and rob houses, rob people."

"And they robbed you?"

"It's kind of a long story."

"Let's hear it, but make it short."

He'd been working for an American's charter service on Ambergris, running tourists out to the reef on snorkeling and scuba diving excursions. A man Tyner's boss knew, an archeologist, needed a boat to take him in the opposite direction—upriver to a remote, unexcavated Mayan ruin near the Guatemalan border. It couldn't be reached otherwise because there were no roads into the place. So, Tyner delivered him, his tools, and supplies in a panga. On the return trip, they were waylaid by river robbers posing as cops. Or maybe they really were cops. Sometimes you couldn't tell the difference in this country. The thugs took their money and vanished. He was happy they didn't steal the panga as well, leaving him and the other man to walk home through miles of jungle. When they made it back to Ambergris, Tyner learned that while he was gone, his boss had left the country—some kind of family emergency—and the local man running the business in his absence refused to advance him the next week's pay.

"So, Covington—the archeologist—promised to wire his museum to wire me some money, but he never did. You want to know the truth?" Leaning forward a little, and half-closing one eye, he whispers, "I don't think he was a real archeologist. One of those dudes who loots tombs and ruins. So, I'm thinking, 'Got to get my young ass out of this ratfuck of a place,' and I went to the bar I told you about because I know the bartender, and I asked him to front me airfare to Anywhere, USA, but he said he didn't have the cash. And I'm thinking, how do I get to the embassy in Belmopan, maybe the embassy will help me with the plane fare. And that's when I overheard this lady, a nurse, I think, talking about you losing a crewman and needing another one."

This colorful tale begs more than a few questions, but Kirby's instincts, that is, his right brain, inclines him to believe it. Tyner could not have made it up, unless he has a screenwriter's imagination.

"Had yourself quite an adventure," he says. "How about you show me some ID."

Tyner fishes a passport from his back pocket and hands it over. The photo and physical description match. The stamps show that he'd entered the country three months ago on an extended visa.

"Can you cook?"

"Hey, that's what I did on the *Ti*."

"No bullshit?"

"None."

"Cause that's what you'll do if you hitch a ride with us. You'll have to get yourself home from Bermuda. The consulate there might help you out."

Tyner's expression brightens. "So, I'm hired?"

"We haven't had breakfast yet. You cook it and if we like it, you're on."

"Give me a few minutes to get my gear."

He's gone considerably longer than a few minutes, returning almost at lunchtime with a denim seabag slung over one scrawny shoulder. His tardiness irritates Kirby, but he forgives Tyner when he explains, apologetically, that the dive shop where he'd stowed his things was closed and he had to wait for the manager to open it.

Breakfast will be brunch. He whips up an omelet on the galley stove, adding Dinty Moore canned beef stew, a splash of hot sauce, chopped red onion, and bell pepper. The meal meets with approval, and he is welcomed aboard. He's polite and affable and the charm of his youth works further into Kirby's psyche. He fills his new crewman in on ship rules: four-hour watches rotating every twelve hours; outgoing watch to brief oncoming on weather, sea conditions, course, and any problems with engine or equipment; oncoming to repeat the course to the off-going; and no one but the captain and the mate permitted to touch *one damn thing* at the nav station.

"That means you. Got all that?"

"Sure," Tyner says, and collects the dishes and starts washing them.

"So, how'd you fetch up in Belize?" Mike asks him.

"Like Gilda Radner said, life is just one thing after another."

"She said that? You look kinda young to have seen Gilda Radner."

"I watched *Saturday Night Live* reruns."

"So, what did you mean, one thing after another?"

"I wanted, like, to see the world. Landed a job with a charter service taking tourists out to the reef, like I said."

"Uh-huh. Kirby told me you brought some archeologist dude. . ."

"Covington."

"What was he looking for? Did those river robbers take whatever it was?"

Tyner shrugs and smiles his disarming smile and says he doesn't have the answers to those questions, he knows nothing about Mayan artifacts, his job had been to bring the guy in and bring him out. His retelling of the tale deepens Kirby's sympathies; he thinks that Mike, looking at their new man through slitted eyes, sounds more like he's conducting an interrogation than satisfying simple curiosity.

The *Cuyahoga* clears out at three in the afternoon, fifteen hundred hours by the nautical clock, her main, jib, and mizzen flown mostly for show because the morning wind has fallen to a spasmodic zephyr. Kirby handles the steering through the deep-water channel, the ancient diesel shuddering below decks and throwing out more blue smoke than he and Mike care for. Twenty minutes under power brings them well out into the Caribbean, where the wind freshens and Kirby shuts the engine to conserve fuel. The vessel, on a beam reach, cruises north by east at a steady seven knots. It pleases him to be out at sea again, all signs of land erased. Mother ocean can kill you or terrify you as much as she can soothe and inspire, but she is never false—she's pure, uncomplicated, unambiguous in her intentions.

They make one hundred sixty-two miles of northing in the first twenty-four hours, and enough in the next twenty-four to pass through the Yucatan Channel. Contrary winds and cross-currents give them a bumpy ride in the channel until they pick up the Loop Current, the part of the Gulf Stream that sweeps through the Gulf of Mexico. With a wind blowing in the direction of its flow, the *Cuyahoga* cracks along very nicely. The log reads eight knots.

At noon of the third day, Kirby turns the helm over to Mike and breaks out his sextant from its rosewood box. A Cassen and Plath, a fusion of form and function. With its black telescope and brass arc, it possesses the aesthetics of precision; it's a *moral* instrument that will never lie to you if used properly. Nor does it depend on electronics and signals from satellites two hundred miles up. He takes a noon sight. Noticing Tyner watching him at this task, he asks if he knows celestial navigation. Tyner shakes his head.

"Care to learn?"

Tyner cants his head to one side and replies he's the cook, not the navigator, and why bother with a sextant when you have GPS? What would you do if the GPS failed? Kirby says. How would you know where you were on the empty, featureless ocean?

"Not a clue. I'm going to make peanut butter and jelly sandwiches for lunch."

Kirby's disappointed; he enjoys teaching advanced skills like celestial navigation to neophytes. But he's getting along with his new crewman. Mike, on the other hand, speaks to him only when absolutely necessary.

"There's something off about that guy," Mike says to Kirby that night. They are in their stateroom, while Tyner stands his trick at the helm.

"Off?" Kirby says. "Off how? Off-color? Off-hand? Off-center?"

Mike, sitting at the table between their berths, rubs a stain with the heel of his hand. "Can't pin it down, but off-center comes close. Him and that story he told about river robbers. Sounds like something out of Huck Finn."

"*That's* what's off about him?" Kirby asks. He's stretched out in his bunk, listening to the low growl of the seas running past the wooden hull.

"All I'm saying is he looks sweet as a new baby goose, but I'm not sure he is."

"We'll do better to talk weather."

"What about the weather?"

"Latest report from NOAA says there's a tropical wave out in the Atlantic. It's strengthening, moving west pretty quick. Should pass to the north of us. But we'll want to keep an eye on it."

Isaac's headlamp illuminated a fer-de-lance, as big around as a strong man's forearm, coiled no more than two yards away. The intrusion of three humans into its lair appeared not to have disturbed it; it lay perfectly motionless, its head, shaped like a spearpoint, resting on its body. The men backed slowly away, Isaac keeping his light on the viper. Then Tyner eased his pack from off one shoulder and reached in for the pistol, and holding it in steady in both hands, fired two quick shots, the buckshot splattering dirt. The fer-de-lance leapt off the ground and writhed in midair like a serpent conjured out of a snake charmer's basket before it fell back to the ground, blood spurting from its eyes, or from the holes where its eyes had been. Its jaws with its twin fangs snapped for a few seconds, as if it didn't know it was dead. Then it lay motionless once again.

"Son of a bitch!" Covington said. His own voice sounded distant, muffled by the ringing in his ears set off by the gunfire in the enclosed space.

"This ain't good, ain't good at all," said Isaac, staring at the snake, stretched out in front of him. It looked to be nearly six feet long. "Never seen no Tommygoff in here before."

"First time for everything," said Tyner. Bending low, he picked up a handful of pebbles and threw them at the fer-de-lance to make sure it was dead. "And this one isn't here anymore."

"Like it's here guardin' things."

"Thought that was the jaguar's job," said Covington, slightly out of breath.

"I'm not likin' it, me. Think we go look for somethin' else. Plenty of stuff here."

Covington turned so that his headlamp shone directly into Isaac's face. "It's this thing I want. I'm paying you good money to bring me to it, so drop the mumbo jumbo and show me where it is."

Isaac paused. The sweat on his forehead and upper lip sparkled in the light. His lip twitched, greed wrestling with dread.

Greed won. He removed his own lamp and fixed its beam on the block with the epitaph to the high priest,

"Thing you want, the statue, behind that there. Maya fella show it to me."

"You left it here. Why?"

"Mebbe fella like you pay more for it than other fellas I'm sellin' to."

"Let's see it, then we'll talk terms."

"Toss me that prybar you got, gimme."

Covington removed the prybar from his pack and handed it to Isaac, who stuck the curved end into a crack between the block and the one beside it, then did the same on the other side so that it came out as easily as the lid to a box. It wasn't a full-size block, but a kind of plaque perhaps two inches thick. Behind it was an alcove, something like a primitive wall safe. He set the plaque on the ground, taking care not to break it.

Covington shined his light into the dark space it had concealed and gave out a low whistle and said, "My, my. My oh my."

Tyner, looking past him into the alcove, asked, "What the hell is that?"

"Pure jade," Covington said, in a hushed voice. "Looks to me like the whole thing's been carved out of jade. Never seen the likes of it."

"What the hell is it?"

"Who. Who is better. He has a dozen names. Ah Puch. Hunhau. Uacmitun. Lord of the Underworld, the god of death. This one. . . . There's collectors who'd strangle their firstborn to get their hands on it."

By the middle of day four, they are cruising through the Florida Straits, roughly sixty-five miles west of Cuba and half that distance east of the Florida Keys. The water is a deep blue shading toward purple, and the sunlight falls through it in beveled planes in which plankton swirl like sparkling dust. A favorable wind has dropped almost to nothing and Kirby starts the antique Perkins that thumps and smokes like the engine on the

African Queen. It and the Gulf current move the boat along at a decent clip. Tyner sprawls on deck forward, either dozing or sunning himself, when a shackle on the limp jib breaks loose, the halyard cracks against the mainmast, and the sail tumbles on top of him, a huge, flapping shroud. He thrashes in a panic until Mike pulls it off.

Kirby lashes the helm to stay on course—the *Cuyahoga*'s autopilot is a corroded relic—then rigs a boatswain's chair to the halyard and Mike hoists him aloft, almost all the way up the mast to reaffix the shackle. After he's lowered to the deck, Kirby resets the sail, though it isn't of much use in the dead air, and resumes steering. The *Cuyahoga* lumbers on over the glittering plain of the sea.

"You're okay?" Kirby asks Tyner.

Tyner's face is almost as white as the sail. "I heard it pop and the next thing I know I'm wrapped up like a fish," he says in an unsteady voice.

"You sure were flopping like one. Go below and get some sleep. That's where you should have been anyway. You're on watch in two hours."

"Man, it's too friggin' hot down there in the V-berth," Tyner whines.

Mike pokes him with a thick, gnarled finger. "Captain says to go below, you go below."

The sun burns like an infrared lamp through a low haze in the west when Kirby's watch ends and Tyner comes up for his turn. Kirby briefs him on the weather, the wind speed and direction, the boat's speed, the course.

Tyner flops down on a cushion and mutters, "Got it."

"You forgot something."

"What?"

"Rule number one when changing watch. The helmsman coming on repeats the course to the one going off."

"Right. What did you say it was?"

"Zero-two-five."

"Okay. Zero-two-five. I'm a little, y'know, sick."

"What kind of sick?"

"Like seasick. It's that V-berth I'm in . . . no air and hot as hell, and I can feel every wave."

"The former owner tore out all the other berths to make room for his contraband, but you can move yourself into the salon, stretch out on one of the cushions in the salon."

He then sends Tyner below to get a Dramamine from the medicine chest. Almost fifteen minutes passes before he returns.

"What the hell took you so long?" Kirby says, annoyed.

"I was taking a look at the charts, the GPS."

"At the nav station? Didn't I brief you that? No one but Mike or me touches *anything* at the nav station."

"I didn't touch nothing," Tyner protests, his tone somewhere between petulant and insolent. He falls silent, turning to gaze over his left shoulder, seemingly at a shearwater flying alongside. "I was wondering . . . I mean . . . Could I ask you a big favor?"

"Ask, but you might not receive."

"It's like this. Florida, Jacksonville, it's right over there, forty, forty-five miles due west." He bows his head slightly, looking askance. "Make a hard turn to port and we'd be there in a few hours and, y'know, you could just sorta drop me off."

Kirby needs several seconds to absorb this outlandish request before he speaks: "*Drop you off*?"

"It's a lot to ask, but. . ."

"This isn't a water taxi."

"Right, but I just thought. . ."

"You signed for a voyage to Bermuda. We've got a long way to go. We're already a couple of days behind schedule, and you *just thought* we could add another day or two to drop you off? Jesus. You've got the con, Tyner. Zero-two-five."

Promptings from his left brain—*maybe there is something off about him*—persuades Kirby to remain above decks while Tyner steers. The sun sets and as night falls, a brisk nor'wester springs up, the engine is killed once again, and the *Cuyahoga*, flying all her canvas, slices through three-foot seas, her bow spitting froth. The boat has a tendency to weather up and Tyner struggles to hold her on a northeasterly course. Kirby, noticing that Tyner's gaze is fastened on the compass, offers a tip in ship handling.

"Stop looking at the compass constantly, that's a mistake because it swings faster than the boat, causing you to oversteer. She's old and rickety, but she's even-tempered and responsive. Needs only a touch. Don't horse her. Pick a star in the north, northeast and steer for it."

"Roger dodger."

"The Dramamine helping?"

Tyner answers that it is.

"That archeologist, tell me again what he was he looking for."

"Jesus, that again? Some kinda Mayan statue. A little Mayan statue, a head and shoulders thing."

"I thought you didn't know what it was."

Tyner doesn't reply immediately. Probably still thinking about a Florida landing—or how to respond. Then he says: "What I meant was that I didn't get a good look at it. He stashed it in his backpack, the archeologist, and I didn't get a good look. It had a weird name. You know anything about Mayan gods?"

"Not a damn thing," Kirby replies. "Mike does. He spent some time in the Yucatan in the way back when."

"Creepy, y'know, those ruins Covington went into. All grown over with jungle. Like something out of *Indiana Jones*."

"Did the robbers steal the backpack?"

"Nope. All they wanted was our money, and they got it. Sure." Tyner pauses, glanced at the compass, then up at the star. "What's with all these questions?"

"Just making conversation."

Kirby goes below, checks the GPS and the charts; then, from the top of the companionway, he orders Tyner to alter course to sixty degrees.

The *Cuyahoga* falls off nicely, Kirby hops to the deck, eases the sheets to all three sails, and when they're drawing well, makes them fast.

They sail on. More than eight hundred miles of ocean now lie ahead, and nothing but ocean, not an island or land of any kind to duck into in the event of bad weather till they sight Bermuda. A half-moon, hovering about halfway between the zenith and the eastern horizon, lays a white stripe on the dark seas and partially illuminates Tyner's profile. Kirby now wonders if the resemblance to his own youthful self had clouded his judgment. He has a thought, quickly dismissed, to grant Tyner's request, come about, detour to the Florida coast. Pull into a marina. Call for a launch to take him ashore. Be done with him.

Mike, rubbing his hairless head and smacking his lips, comes up to stand his trick. Tyner all but runs below to his berth. Just before he turns in, Kirby glances at the logbook and observes that their new shipmate, in his rush to curl up in his bunk, had committed another violation of regulations: he'd failed to enter essential information, which included the *Cuyahoga*'s location at the time when he went off watch. Kirby fills in the data for him. Too worn out to reprimand him now. Save that till tomorrow. He then tunes into the NOAA weather report on the single sideband. The tropical wave has intensified to a full gale, acquiring the name Tropical Storm Ginger. It's northeast of Bermuda, tracking due west toward North Carolina. The bad news: winds are expected to reach hurricane force before daylight. The good news: Ginger is predicted to turn north and blow itself out in the colder waters off New England.

Covington slipped on a pair of surgical gloves, and with great care removed the jade icon from the alcove. It was the figure of some half-human thing about a foot high, seated with its green knees drawn up into its green, bloated belly. Its face had slanted eyes and a long, flat nose above thick, partly open lips and a collar decorated with what looked like tiny eyes encircled its neck. A symbol of some kind, carved into the statue's forehead, had Covington's attention. He shined his light on it and whistled again, muttering about the remarkable state of preservation.

"See this? It's Akbal, the emblem of darkness. You might say it's the death god's calling card, the ace of spades."

"What did you mean about collectors cutting their mother's throats?" asked Tyner.

"I said strangle their first born. This workmanship is incredible. Jade is hard to carve, only the best artisans worked with it." He pulled a bolt of burlap from his pack and wrapped it around the statue twice, three times, like a salesclerk wrapping some fragile, expensive object. "This one, it's worth a fortune."

"How big this fortune?" Isaac inquired as Covington placed the statue in his pack.

"We'll see. We'll see after my customer gets a look and bids," he said.

Isaac kicked the dead snake aside. They walked out of the shaft into the jungle where sunlight fell through the trees in slanted pillars. "You and me we got a deal, us."

"I know that."

"I'll be spectin' for you to make good on your end."

"I will."

"You don't, and this the last time you get in here, this thing the last thing you bring out. You try and you see what happens to you."

Covington spread his arms as if welcoming a lost friend into his home. "Hey, bro, you have nothing to. . ."

"I ain't your 'bro'," Isaac said.

Day six. The nor'wester has gone into retirement, replaced by a dead calm that transforms the previously bumpy seas into a blue mirror, barely a ripple on it. The sails droop, and under what power the creaky Perkins can provide, the *Cuyahoga* chugs on at about two knots. Tyner is steering. Kirby, taking a noon sight with his sextant, doesn't like the look of the skies—blemished by high, wispy cirrus arranged in ragged lines, like the bars on a mackerel's flanks. He recalls an old sailor's aphorism: Mackerel skies and mare's tails, tall-masted ships shorten their sails.

Below decks, he finds Mike seated at the nav station, a nautical chart spread on the table, another glowing on the GPS screen in front of him. The single sideband crackles. The previous owner, shoddy as he'd been on maintenance, had installed first-rate electronics, those required for a successful smuggling operation. Too bad he hadn't been as conscientious about the engine and the autopilot.

"Ginger's changed course, she's now headed southwest," Mike says, pointing at the screen.

"*What*?"

"I said it's. . ."

"I heard you. That doesn't compute. NOAA reported that steering currents were pushing it north."

"We both know that tracking hurricanes isn't a precise art," Mike says. He taps a pencil on their current rhumb line, drawn on the paper chart, then presses a finger on the storm's position, and with his thumb traces an arc southwestward. "It's traveling at ten knots, NOAA says. We're bearing northeast, sixty degrees, at two. It crosses our path right about here." Tapping the pencil again. "In two days at most. Sooner if it picks up speed."

Kirby squints at the chart. "Meaning we'd better change course ourselves. Come up to a few degrees east of due north. Worst that can happen then is we hit the outer bands."

"You didn't get your captain's license for nothing."

"Fuck you. Zero two zero should do it. Agreed?"

Kirby scrambles up to the cockpit and orders Tyner to come up to the new heading.

"What for?" Tyner says.

"Because I fucking told you to!"

They have covered only ten miles in four hours, the engine smoking worse than ever, when, to everyone's gratitude, a light but steady breeze starts to blow out of the north and they are able to stop running under power. Close-hauled, the *Cuyahoga* beats on at six knots steady. Kirby calculates the storm will pass well south of them; they should reach a waypoint west of Bermuda in three days, assuming they maintain their current speed, and bear off from there to the island.

He of all people ought to know better than to make happy predictions. Late in the afternoon, Ginger changes direction a second time, hooking from southwest to almost due west while gaining strength and picking up speed to thirteen knots. Even the NOAA reporter, who customarily speaks in a robotic voice, utters this announcement with a distinct note of surprise.

The *Cuyahoga* is once again on a collision course with the erratic storm. "Like Mitch, it's like Mitch," Kirby says, naming the hurricane that zigzagged all over the Bay of Campeche in 1998 and sent the windjammer *Fantome* to the bottom with all thirty-one hands. That ship's captain had done all he could to avoid the Category 5 monster, but it seemed to possess intent, seemed to guess his moves every time, leaving him with nowhere to run or hide. Kirby now feels that he and his crew are in a similar situation.

"What do you think, Mike?" he asks, attempting not to sound too nervous. "We can't outrun it."

Mike gazes at the GPS, then down at the chart, as though to wring an answer out of them. "Head back south? Dead run due south, heave to, and wait for the storm to blow out of our path, give us a clear shot to Bermuda."

Kirby's mind raced. Ginger's eyewall is about two hundred miles from the *Cuyahoga's* present position. It's now a Category 2, with hurricane force winds extending well away from the eye in all directions.

"Light airs like this we won't get that far," Kirby says.

He gestures to Mike to give him his seat. He plops down with a parallel rule and protractor and dividers and begins to make time and distance calculations on a notepad, his left brain totally engaged.

"We fall off to the east," he said when he's done. "Heading one zero zero. We probably won't avoid Ginger completely, but if it keeps on the direction it's going, we'll miss her completely at best, at worst, we catch the outer bands on the backside. . ."

"Where the winds are weakest," Mike says.

"Yup. We start prep now. We'll be in dirty weather pretty damn soon."

"What's going on?" Tyner asks when Kirby takes the wheel and brings the *Cuyahoga* over to her new heading. She is now on a broad reach and making seven knots.

"Dodging a hurricane," he answers.

Panic flickers in the deep blue eyes.

"Give Mike a hand trimming sail."

"We're going to miss it, aren't we?"

"Sure will give it a try. Now hop to it and help Mike and from now on you do exactly as I say, no questions."

They all don foul-weather gear and strap on safety harnesses; then, with the wheel lashed again, they lower the mizzen and mainsails. Furling the main is hazardous, requiring them to clip the safety harnesses to jacklines while they balance on the slick deckhouse and cinch tie wraps around the boom, swinging like an open gate. Urgency in their every move, they shuttle loose objects on deck below, even the cockpit seat cushions, dog hatchways, lash galley cabinets with bungee cord, and inspect the case in which the life raft is packed, to make sure it's ready for deployment should the worst happen.

Later, the wind rises to twenty-five knots—a half-gale and then some. The *Cuyahoga*, heeling hard to starboard, presses on, powered by a double-reefed jib. Each man takes two-hour turns at the wheel. Tyner looks apprehensive, if not downright terrified, when the aging vessel slides down a wave and bangs into the trough, rattling like a junk wagon.

The disaster happens near nightfall: an electrical fire. Sparks crackle from the bulkhead behind the nav station, wisps of smoke curl out from the instruments. Immediately, the radio goes silent, the GPS dark. Mike rushes forward for a fire extinguisher bolted to a bulkhead in the V-berth, while Kirby, pitched to-and-fro by the pitching of the ship, loosens the panel screws and pulls out the single sideband and the GPS units. Smoke billows from both, expelling the stink of fried insulation and copper and burned terminals. Mike stumbles along the passageway with the extinguisher, aims the nozzle at the smoking wires, pulls the pin, depresses the lever, and. . .

"What the fuck! It's empty!"

"There's another one in the engine room!" Kirby yells.

Mike comes back with a bleeding golf ball on his forehead, having struck an overhead stringer with his skull—the engine room is more a low-ceilinged compartment than a room. A great, satisfying plume of fire retardant blows from the nozzle and covers the burned units in foam. Mike shoves the nozzle into the cavity between the bulkhead and the hull to snuff any hidden flames. He sprays till the extinguisher is empty.

Kirby leans against the chart table and gazes dumbly at the guts of the radio and the GPS, charred beyond repair.

"I knew the electrical in this goddamn. . ." Mike begins.

"We've still got a sextant and compass," Kirby says, putting as positive a spin on things as he can. "That's all sailors had for four hundred years."

"Great, we get to play Christopher Columbus. No radio, no idea what the storm is doing, and if we get into trouble. . ."

They feel the *Cuyahoga* rise on a sea, plunge, and roll as the next sea surges under her. The faulty extinguisher slides backward then forward on the floor. Kirby looks at it quizzically. He could swear that the extinguisher in the V-berth forward was red and thin, like the one aft, in the engine room; this one is white and twice the thickness. He picks it up, noticing as he does that the pressure gauge needle is fixed on recharge, as if it had been used, yet it feels full, feels in fact unusually heavy. Holding it in both hands, he shakes it and hears something rattle inside, then observes another odd thing: a band of lumpy metal such as might be made by a welder's torch midway between the extinguisher's neck and its bottom. The weld has been painted over in a crude, or hurried, attempt to disguise it.

Listening to his right brain, he goes aft to the tool chest stowed in a drawer and returns with a small hacksaw and begins cutting into the weld. Mike asks what the hell is he doing? Kirby doesn't answer and continues to saw in a circle, taking care not to cut too deeply. He finishes, pulls the two halves apart and removes from inside a small, greenish statue about a foot high. It has a bulging belly and an ugly but exquisitely carved face.

"Well, holy shit," Mike says, moving to sit next to Kirby. "Holy living shit."

"Know what it is?"

Mike takes it in his hands, turns it around, strokes it with his fingers, and shakes his head.

"It's a Mayan god or idol. And pure jade. Beyond that, couldn't say."

"I was wrong about him. You were right, Mike," Kirby says. "Think if we search his berth we'll find the extinguisher that came with boat."

It is under a pile of life jackets in a compartment beneath the portside bunk. That isn't all they find. A semi-automatic pistol with two rounds in the magazine is stashed in Tyner's seabag, along with an address book containing names and phone numbers and a sticker on the inside of the front cover that reads, "Property of E. L. Covington. If found, contact. . ." and a memory stick that presumably contains a digital record of the address book.

"Take the helm, Mike, and tell him to come below, but don't tell him why."

Tyner, wearing an expression part sheepish and part defiant, sits on one side of the dining table, Kirby opposite him, with the pistol shoved into his belt and the idol on the table, his palm clamped over it to prevent it from tumbling onto the floor.

"So, you're not going to explain how this managed to crawl inside a fire extinguisher?" Kirby asks, calmly. "You're not going to explain why you bullshitted me and Mike? You're not going to explain what you're doing with a gun and this Covington guy's address book?"

"I don't owe you any explanations," Tyner replies, his hands clasped under his chin, his lips curled into something between a pout and a sneer.

"But you do. Sure you do."

Tyner is silent. Unclasping his hands, he grips both sides of the table as the *Cuyahoga* rolls again, a sharp, sudden roll to port, then to starboard, followed by a lift on a sea.

"Okay, I'll explain it for you," Kirby says. "You stole this little beauty from Covington."

"He didn't own it. He stole it himself."

"Right. A thief robbing a thief. Then, after I gave you the okay to come aboard and you went to get your gear, you were gone a long while. You somehow or other got hold of that fire extinguisher, cut it in half, stashed the artifact inside, and swapped it for the one that was already on board. I guess the idea was that customs in Bermuda might search the boat when we clear in, but they'd be unlikely to look into a fire extinguisher. Don't know what you planned to do after that. Maybe you didn't have a plan except that you were going to get hold of a contact in Covington's address book, sell the goods to him. There are a lot of gaps that need filling, but that's the overall picture. What do you have to say?"

Kirby tilts his head slightly to prompt an answer. Tyner doesn't give one.

"So, what happened to Mr. Covington?"

"He's alright. So is Isaac."

"Isaac? Who the fuck is Isaac?"

"A dude who brought us to the ruins," Tyner replies sullenly. "They're both all right. Hey, Kirby, I didn't kill them if that's what you're driving at, so you can stop coming off like a cop because you're not one."

"You're right again! But I am the skipper of this vessel, and that gives me the power to confiscate your little treasure and the gun. Also to confine you to quarters. The V-berth. Get your ass up and in there."

Tyner hesitates, as if pondering Kirby's command, starts to rise, then drops back to his seat.

"Daddy is sending me to my room for a time-out?"

"That's where you'll be unless we call for you. We might need a third hand if this storm gets any worse." Kirby stands, unsteady in the rocking, plunging boat, and lowers his hand to the butt of the pistol. "You're not going to make me force you at gunpoint, are you?"

"That depends on if you've got the nerve to use it."

This insolent, defiant Tyner is so different from the Tyner who'd begged his way aboard days ago as to be another personality altogether.

"There's one way for you to find out," Kirby says.

Tyner rises abruptly, and grins. "I'll be a good boy and do what daddy says."

For the better part of the night, Kirby and Mike spell each other at the helm and the task of making sure Tyner stays put in the forward berth. The wind is blowing at better than thirty-five knots—a whole gale. Maybe, Kirby thinks, he'd erred by confronting Tyner with his discovery. Maybe he should have saved all that for when they put into Bermuda harbor. No point in second guessing himself. You did what you did, he says to himself. Live with it.

Now, with a second reef in the jib, the vessel plows through frothing seas of twelve to fourteen feet. Kirby tries to guess where Ginger is headed, the location of its eye. He reviews everything he's learned about hurricanes and the forces that determine its path—steering currents, high-pressure ridges, the jet stream—all of which are unknown to him because the radio and nav equipment are shot. So that, too, is pointless. Ragged clouds scud across the black sky, spindrifts twirl from the crests of the waves, which sometimes send sheets of green water over the deck. He can determine his own position only by dead-reckoning, but that does not, cannot, tell him if they're going to pass safely through the outer bands, or, if the storm has undergone another unexpected change in direction, they are sailing into its howling heart.

The second catastrophe strikes an hour or two before dawn, not long after the *Cuyahoga* has crashed into a deep trough with such force that it all but knocks Kirby off his feet. He's on watch, Mike and Tyner below. He hears Tyner scream: "Flooding! There's a flood in my berth!" Leaving the wheel tightly snubbed, he rushes below and finds Mike lying in an inch or two of seawater, with his arm plunged into an open hatch from which more water gushes out and sweeps across the decking in a thin, sickening sheet.

"A through-hull failed," he says to Kirby, breathless "Bilge pump hose popped loose, I can feel it, and I'm pretty sure a couple of planks sprang loose with the pounding we've been taking, the last one especially." He pauses. "I probably can bung the through-hull, but there's nothing we can do about the sprung planks."

"We can shove stuff down in there. Pillows, blankets, that can buy us some time. Tyner, there's a five-gallon bucket aft. Get it, start bailing."

"She won't live," Mike says, swiping his brow with a wet forearm. "She's going down."

Panic rises in Kirby's throat, like a lump of vomit. Tyner runs in with the bucket, fills it, and runs out, but slips on a companionway step. The water he intended to toss overboard sloshes over the floor. The mishap cures Kirby's bout of nerves.

"Forget that, Tyner. Get a life vest. Mike, with me."

Outside, in what feels like fifty knots of wind, he and Mike crawl on hands and knees over the deckhouse roof to the life raft case, pop it loose, and drag it into the cockpit, where there is less danger of being swept overboard. Mike ties the painter to a cleat, then tosses the raft into the sea. The painter pays out some twenty-five yards. Both men haul in the slack, and when it comes taut, give it a sharp tug. The case breaks open and the bright orange raft, big enough for six people, inflates with a hiss of CO2.

"It worked, thank you God for small favors," Mike says at a yell.

Standard practice is to remain on a stricken vessel as long as possible before abandoning ship. Kirby knows that won't be very long when he goes below to retrieve the logbook. The water in the main cabin is ankle deep and rising quickly and spilling into his and Mike's stateroom. He is shocked to see Tyner in there, furiously turning over seat cushions, opening drawers.

"Goddamnit, get in your life jacket!" he shouts.

"Where is it? Where the fuck is it . . . ?"

"There's a whole pile of them in. . ." Kirby begins, stopping himself when he realizes Tyner isn't referring to a life jacket.

"It's worth a fortune!" Tyner yells back.

Kirby tears a jacket from a locker next to the nav station and tosses it at Tyner. The power of greed to overcome almost every human need and desire, even survival, ought not to amaze him, but it does. The water has already risen halfway to his knees. The sprung planks in the bow must have given way, creating a hole the size of a trash can lid. He grabs the logbook—it will be necessary in an inquiry—and returns to the cockpit, where Mike stands with one leg below the other, gripping the wheel with both hands. The *Cuyahoga* is beginning to list. Gray clouds race low over a gray sea. Spume flies over the waves and the sea becomes a roiling fogbank. The vessel gives a sudden lurch to starboard and remains there, her rail underwater.

"In! Now!" he cries out to Mike, then, yelling to Tyner to come topside, follows Mike over the rail into the raft. The *Cuyahoga* lists further, she's at forty degrees or better, close to rolling over on her beam ends. If she does, she'll crush the raft.

"TYNER!!"

It's doubtful he can hear Kirby over the wind.

Kirby opens a clasp knife attached to a lanyard and cuts the painter and the raft and the *Cuyahoga* drift apart. Tyner appears on deck, which is nearly vertical now, and he's on his belly and clinging to the port rail. That is the last Kirby sees of him. The ship's bow buries itself in a sea and she tumbles onto her side, her mast tilting far over before she vanishes.

With water dripping from the hood of his foul-weather jacket, Mike stares at the spot where the *Cuyahoga* sank.

"God almighty," he says softly. "But it was us or him. Right? It was us or him."

Remembering the jib halyard snapping for no reason and the hurricane's unpredictable meanderings and the fire destroying the radio and GPS and the failure of the through-hull fitting and the sprung planks, Kirby's right brain forms a judgment that he does not speak: Tyner was a Jonah if ever he saw one.

"That's right," he says. "Us or him."

COILS OF THE PAST

They were walking through the village cemetery, its tombs freshly whitewashed, some bearing calligraphic inscriptions from the time before the French imposed the Roman alphabet on the country, when a flock of birds rose from behind a low hill and circled and swooped, making distressful cries.

"Plovers," Marion declared firmly, and defended her identification by calling attention to the black and white striping on their throats, their long, slender legs and pointed tails. "They're almost identical to Killdeer."

Back home in Arizona, she volunteered for a local chapter of the Audubon Society, leading bird counts during the seasonal migrations to and from Mexico. Her husband, Timothy Fellowes, and his friend, whose name is Rob Jenter, each muttered an "uh-huh" in deference to her expertise. Fellowes was impressed by the abundant bird life they'd seen so far—green and turquoise songbirds, waterfowl, egrets with wings white as fresco angels, and now plovers. He could not remember ever seeing birds of any species during the war. They must have been around, of course; probably, he hadn't noticed, being focused entirely on staying alive.

"I guess we've disturbed their nesting area," Marion speculated. "That's why they're making those cries."

"I do not think so," said Tráng, their guide, interpreter, and minder, the latter being his primary job. The regime in Hanoi had liberalized a good deal in the past decade, but not so much that it could allow foreigners to wander around unsupervised.

"You don't think they would make their nests here?" Marion asked.

"Oh, I don't know. But you see, not all the dead here lie in the ground."

With a half-grin on her thin lips, Marion squinted with one eye. "I'm afraid I don't understand."

Tráng, who stood about five-feet-five and wore an olive-drab pith helmet, pointed at the plovers, flying round and round. "Those are the souls of the dead from the war, both Vietnamese and American, and they are crying out their sorrow to the living."

Marion looked at him, perplexed. He'd made his identification in the same firm, unequivocal way she had made hers. Then he said, "*Hãy để chúng tôi bắt đầu.*"

"Roger that," said Jenter, who spoke Vietnamese.

Tráng led them down a footpath back to the road, then went off toward a row of soft drink and tea stalls to find their van and its driver. The day was as hot as Fellowes remembered from many years ago, more years than he cared to count. He felt as though he was breathing through a mask made of warm, damp ClingWrap. There were other reasons for his labored breaths, but they had nothing to do with the climate.

"What a weird thing for him to say, that the plovers are souls of the dead," Marion remarked.

"He's a poet," her husband said. "Didn't he tell us that he's a published poet? Poets say weird things."

"He wasn't speaking poetically. Like it's a fact, like he believed it."

"He probably does," Jenter said. He fanned himself with his baseball cap and turned to look up the road. "The van can't get here soon enough. A blast of AC. . ."

"Why would he believe such nonsense, an educated, intelligent man?"

"Because it isn't nonsense to him," answered Jenter impatiently. "They don't make the sorts of distinctions we do. The supernatural world is as real to them as the one you can see and smell and touch."

Marion's eyebrows arched; a pained, slightly disdainful look came over her long face. She'd been a professor of biology and was quite sure that there was no world but the one of see-smell-touch. Fellowes was a practicing Catholic, an usher at St. Augustine Cathedral in Tucson. He and Marion had been married thirty-eight years, had raised three children, and were still in love in spite of their differences. Or perhaps because of them. Their frequent, sometimes acrimonious, sometimes friendly, but always lively debates on his faith versus her materialism had been—still were—a preventative to marital boredom.

The white van with the company name on its doors in blue—South Asia Excursions— finally came down the road. Tráng hopped out and opened the sliding door. Fellowes, Marion, and Jenter squeezed into a rear seat and collectively sighed their relief in the air conditioner's icy gusts. Fellowes marveled that he'd once been able to slog through rice paddies and hump jungled hills in temperatures like this in a fifteen-pound flak jacket while carrying a forty-pound pack and an eight-pound rifle, with spare magazines (five pounds), a one-hundred-round belt of machine gun ammo (five point six pounds) draped over his shoulders, and two full canteens (four pounds) belted to his waist. He'd gone to war weighing one-seventy-five and came home so skinny that his kid brother, Jake, nicknamed him "Flyrod." But he'd gained another kind of weight, which couldn't be measured on a scale and which he'd borne for nearly half a century. He hoped to shed it on this journey back to the places where he'd seen things best left unseen and done things best left undone.

Jenter, a VA counselor, took veterans on trips back to former battlefields twice a year, and had convinced Fellowes to join him on the next one. It would, he promised, ease the burden of memory. Or at least begin to.

Fellowes thought of it as a pilgrimage, and each stop as a kind of shrine. He wanted to make friends with himself, wanted to once again be at peace with himself. In the past three days, wearing the same canvas-and-leather combat boots he'd worn forty-six years ago, he'd walked the same paddy dikes he'd walked then, the same muddy trails once sown with mines and booby-traps. He'd traveled to the hill, marked on military maps as "Hill

44," where a soldier named Keane had been shot through the head by a sniper; he'd revisited the village where, in predawn darkness, he'd shot an infiltrator, discovering when first light came that it was a twelve-year-old kid who'd been collecting empty cans from the company trash pit; he'd stood at the foot of the bridge upon which Paige, his best buddy, had been vaporized by a booby-trapped 250-pound bomb.

Now, he was headed for a village called Ahn Loi, the last shrine on the itinerary, the place he dreaded most to see again and needed most to see because he dreaded it. It was there that some cherished image of himself, already in tatters after nine months in combat, had finally come apart.

Tráng turned around in the front seat and, facing him, presented a half-smile. "Okay, Tim. Close your eyes and tell us how much farther."

Two days ago, searching for the village where he'd shot the twelve-year-old, they had gotten lost. At a crossroad, Tráng and Pham, the driver, asked a farmer for directions, but he was of no help. They turned to Fellowes. Should they go left or right or straight on? He was at a loss; nothing looked familiar. In a moment, he realized why: all his memories of the war were in black and white, but everywhere around him were colors—the emerald rice paddies, the brightly-painted houses and pagodas, the brilliant birds. He shut his eyes, and images played back in his mind like footage from an old newsreel. Gray mud, a leaden monsoon sky, drab huts, the pagodas dingy from age and neglect. He sat as if in a meditative trance, then opened his eyes and said, "Go straight for three or four kilometers. You'll come to the village gate—two stone pillars with a bamboo arch over them. A schoolhouse will be on the left side."

And that is what happened, except that the distance was six kilometers. Everyone was impressed, particularly Tráng, who thought that the tall, aging American had mystical powers.

"I can't do it on cue," Fellowes said to him now, unable to keep the irritation out of his voice. It was as though he'd been asked to do a parlor trick for everyone's entertainment.

"Of course," said Tráng, his smile fading.

Three and a half miles, three point seven to be precise. Fellowes had been an engineer at Raytheon and believed in numbers and equations and geometric theorems as a priest believes in dogma. They were unambiguous, they did not lie or deceive, they'd been his salvation until his retirement last year. Not long afterward, the things best left unseen and undone began to recrudesce; his moods underwent radical changes, morbid silences alternated with outbursts of temper, shaking him like bouts of chronic malaria. Waking up late one night, Marion saw that he was not in bed and went downstairs, where she'd found him sitting in the TV room with the pieces of a revolver in his lap. He'd told her he'd disassembled it because he'd been thinking of shooting himself and figured that he would be less likely to if he had to reassemble the gun first. She clamped a hand over her mouth and asked through her spread fingers what was troubling him, what was so wrong that he'd been, Oh my God, considering suicide? He answered that he didn't know, although he did. What he didn't know then, and still did not, was how to tell her the way he'd felt, looking at the body of a twelve-year-old boy hanging on a barbed wire fence like a piece of blown trash, knowing he'd killed him, and what it had been like to see his best friend blasted into a red mist. He had absolutely no idea how he could ever confess what had happened at Ahn Loi.

Four kilometers now. Multiply by 0.621 = 2.48 miles.

They passed two women walking the roadside with a steady, rhythmic gait, wicker baskets full of sweet potatoes swinging from the ends of their shoulder poles. Motorbikes sped by, raising misty curtains of laterite dust. Fellowes gazed across the paddy lands toward the Truong Son mountains, brooding and mysterious in the distance, and of a green so dark they were almost black. At the front of the range, Núi Chúa, which meant Lord Mountain, rose steeply from foothills blanketed in elephant grass and scrub jungle. It was shaped like a truncated pyramid and was a little more than a mile high. During the war, everyone in Fellowes's company had heard the tale: The ruins of an old French resort, which none of them had seen, stood on the mountain's flat summit. It had been a refuge from the sweltering lowlands for the rubber planters and merchants and officials who had kept the imperial gears turning. The weather up there, amid mists and clouds, was said to be as cool as springtime. The resort became a legend, a tantalizing myth, a Shangri-La that inspired daydreams. He remembered the times when he and Paige, during a break on patrol or on watch in a foxhole, would look at the mountain with longing and entertain themselves with fanciful climbs to the summit to discover if the myth was real; they would imagine themselves, cold beers in their hands, relaxing in a decrepit villa in the refreshing mists and clouds.

He had told Tráng about the Lost Resort, and learned that it did in fact exist, and what was more, that a new one was to be built on its ruins.

"I want to see it," Fellowes had said. "Can you arrange that?"

Tráng replied that he could. A road was being cut along the winding track upon which, a very long time ago, coolies had carried colonial ladies and gentlemen on sedan chairs.

"But we can ride up in the van."

"I'll walk it."

"Tim!" said Tráng, rhyming his name with "team." "The road is fifteen kilometers to the top."

Fellowes did the mental arithmetic. Fifteen kilometers equaled nine point three miles. "I'll do it," he said with emphasis. "I have to."

The climb was scheduled for tomorrow morning. Marion, Jenter, and Tráng would ride up in the van—"a support and rescue vehicle," as Jenter had described it.

Ahn Loi faced a wide river, and the river was just about the only thing he recognized. Houses of stuccoed concrete block had replaced the palm-thatch and bamboo shacks he remembered. Power lines marched across the countryside, delivering the blessings and curses of electricity to places once lit only by oil lamps. Satellite dishes sprouted from a few rooftops. The transformation disoriented him, and he felt like a Rip Van Winkle.

The van dropped them off at the headquarters of the Ahn Loi People's Committee, that is, the town hall, a spacious, sunny, two-story building with a large portrait of Ho Chi Minh overlooking the main room. The travelers met the village chairman and several other people whose functions in local government were not clear but who appeared to be personages of note. The bespectacled, gray-haired chairman served his American guests tea and invited them to dinner that evening. The cordial welcome further disoriented Fellowes; he didn't expect it, didn't think he deserved it. Marion and Jenter, yes, but not him. They drank their tea and exchanged anodyne pleasantries with their hosts, after which an older woman wearing her hair in a tight bun led them to their quarters in an upstairs room. A ceiling fan made a gallant if somewhat ineffective effort to relieve the heat. Four cots shrouded by mosquito nets had been prepared. An outdoor shower—no hot water, but who needed it?—and an indoor toilet delighted Marion. No squatting in the bushes tonight!

Jenter and Tráng decided to take a nap, Fellowes a walk.

"I'll join you," Marion said.

Her face fell when he shook his head, shook it emphatically. "There's something I need to do by myself, you don't mind."

"Actually, I do. But go ahead. I'll find some way to amuse myself."

Westerners were rarely if ever seen in Ahn Loi. The pale-complected, six-foot-two-inch American walking the river road with a determined stride drew curious stares from adults going about their daily tasks, and from the children, who mobbed him, letting out uninhibited squeals and laughter. They were very charming, grabbing his hands, plucking at his pants, calling out in the only English they knew. Hah-lo! Goo-bye! He shooed them off and lengthened his stride and in five or ten minutes came to the western edge of the village, where he sat down, sweat dripping from the rim of his baseball cap. A short distance upstream, the river oxbowed around a broad, table-topped hill, Hill 62. The number designated its height in meters. Multiply by 3.28 = 203.4 feet. Fellowes closed his eyes. . .

The vegetation covering the slopes vanishes, trees and brush having been cut down or burned off to clear fields of fire; howitzer barrels poke from sunken gun pits; foxholes and rolls of concertina wire, like huge, barbed bracelets, encircle the perimeter. This is Firebase Zulu, where Fellowes's company provides security for a battery of one-oh-fives. Below, on a scrubby peninsula formed by the oxbow bend, stalls with sheet-metal roofs and walls composed of flattened beer cans have sprung up to provide the troops with sodas and beer and black-market cigarettes, with soap and plastic soap dishes and military gear like canteens and webbed belts and rucksacks pilfered from the docks in Danang. The war's ghosts draw closer. Fellowes can see them. His machine gun team—Harris, who has replaced Keane as team leader, Mackey, who has replaced Paige as gunner, and himself, the assistant gunner and ammo humper, who so far hasn't been replaced, a circumstance that could be changed in a single flaming instant on the next patrol—are on a resupply mission for their company. They stock up on Camels, Salems, Lucky Strikes to supplement the stale cigarettes issued in C-Ration boxes, load Budweiser cases into the jeep, and are getting set to leave when Harris spots the woman emerging from her bath in the river. Her hair, midnight-black, falls wet over her bare breasts and to her waist. She is wearing only a pair of light-colored panties, which cling to her like a second skin. "*Hey, Cô! Cô đẹp hoa*!" Harris calls out, and the woman, who appears to be in her twenties, is suddenly aware of her nakedness. Snatching the silk pants and áo *dài* she's left on the riverbank, she ducks into a shed half-hidden by bushes. . .

The sound of shrill children's chatter woke him out of this dream that was not a dream; nor was it a memory, a revisiting, rather. His eyes snapped open, and he stood, startling four raggedly dressed boys as they popped out of the reeds and rushes lining the riverbank. The three spun on their heels and fled the instant they saw the lanky stranger with the big nose and sun reddened face. The fourth, who wore a bowl haircut and mud-spattered T-shirt, stood frozen in terror. "Don't be afraid," Fellowes murmured softly, but his words had an effect opposite to what he intended: the kid let out a howl, he screamed as if in a nightmare. His reaction, so starkly different from the reactions of the other children in the village, unnerved Fellowes. Did the boy and his friends know? Was the woman their grandmother or an old aunt or a neighbor and had she told them about the terrible men with big noses and reddened faces and what had happened to her? Was he a kind of bogeyman come to life? The kid screamed again, then overcame his paralysis and ran after the other boys. Suddenly, the air pressure seemed to drop precipitously, the humidity to rise, as before a violent thunderstorm. Fellowes himself wanted to run, but now it was he who couldn't move.

"Ah, so here you are," Marion said from behind him. "Sorry, I followed you, but I. . ."

She fell silent when he turned around and lowered his head a little, breathing deeply through his nostrils, like a runner who has finished a race.

"Are you all right?" she asked, concern wrinkling her forehead.

He made a fluttering movement with one hand.

"What does that mean?"

"I'm okay."

"You don't look it, you look like you've seen a. . ."

Fellowes snorted. "I saw more than one," he said, and immediately wished he'd kept quiet; the statement only piqued her curiosity.

She cocked her chin, curled her tongue against the back of her upper teeth, as she habitually did when an understanding came to her.

"Something happened here. What?"

"Nothing. It's. . ."

"Please don't tell me it's nothing." Her gaze wandered in a circle from his face to the hill to the river and back to him. "You wanted me to make this trip, and I agreed because I care about you. I've stomped around with you for three whole days, going on four, and we stop at some place—that schoolhouse back there, that bridge—and it doesn't look special but seems to mean something to you, but you don't say what or why. You get all silent and weird and locked up inside yourself, like you are now."

He made no comment.

"There! See! Mister Closemouthed! This isn't my idea of a vacation, y'know. Flying halfway around the world so we can tour the countryside with a poet who thinks birds are human spirits and having to pee and crap in the bushes and sweating my sixty-five-year-old ass off. Jenter has some idea that all this is supposed to do you some good, but I don't see that it is."

With one hand he stroked her hair, tinted to its original light brown. He could see the gray roots. She was right—returning to the scenes where his young self had been shredded wasn't doing him any good. It wasn't doing *them* any good. He spoke his deepest fear: "Marion . . . I . . . I don't want to lose you."

"How nice to hear that," she said, not without sarcasm. "Goddamnit, Tim, you haven't been yourself for the last year. I come downstairs in the middle of the night and find you taking a gun apart because you're afraid you'll shoot yourself. I feel like I'm losing *you*."

"You don't want to hear it."

"How do you know what I want or don't want to hear?"

"Because I know you."

"Maybe not as well as you think."

An old man with a stringy goatee rang the bell on his bicycle. They moved aside to allow him to pass. A complicated emotion, resolve mixed with resignation and some anger, surged through Fellowes. *She says she wants to hear, does she? We'll see about that, yeah, I guess we'll see.*

"Let's walk," he said.

The hill that he knew as Firebase Zulu was less than a quarter of a mile away. When they got to it, he found a path that wound away from the hill and down an embankment to the peninsula formed by the oxbow in the river. A big log, probably deposited there during the monsoon floods, lay near the river's edge. He and Marion sat down and watched a young man with the torso of a bantamweight fighter, harnessed to a small sampan attached to a raft laden with sugar cane, wade downstream. Evening was approaching, the blessed hour when the sun lifted its curse; farmers in the fields on the far side were trudging homeward, flicking the haunches of their water buffalo with long bamboo switches.

"During the war, some locals had set up, you could call them concession stands, not too far from where we're sitting," Fellowes began. "This area was pretty quiet, and brigade cut our company some slack, tasked us with guarding the firebase, because we'd been in a lot of shit for three months. We'd lost around fifty dead and wounded out of a hundred and forty."

Without further preamble, he described what had happened to his sergeant, Keane— "I was so dazed that I said something to him and then I saw that half his head was gone"—and shooting the boy he'd mistaken for an infiltrator in the twilight before sunrise—"I dry heaved, the poor kid was scavenging the crap we'd thrown away"—and seeing Paige instantaneously transformed into a red mist by the booby-trapped bomb—"We called it 'getting plumed.'" He spoke in a flat, calm voice, as if he were reading a report written by someone else, for he had been someone else all those years ago, a nineteen-year-old drafted into a war that everyone in that year of 1970 knew could not be won. Finally, in the same almost indifferent tone and in a single sentence, he told her about what Harris and Mackey and he had done to the woman who'd been bathing in the river—"*this* river." He hesitated and looked at his wife, who looked back at him not with horror or revulsion but with incomprehension, as if he'd related to her events on some ghastly planet in another solar system. "Harris went first and then Mackey," he continued. "They told me to stand guard, and I did. I stood guard. Then Harris told me, 'Your turn, PFC Fellowes. One for all and all for one.' I knew what he meant—if we were all guilty, no one would snitch. They had her in some kind of shed, a shed on bamboo poles with old GI helmet liners on the tops of the poles, and I didn't want to do it, couldn't have even if I'd wanted to, I was so scared. Scared sick. I knew it was wrong, but I was more scared of Harris— he was a hero, had won a Silver Star and was one tough dude, ex–Golden Gloves boxer, and my team leader besides. So, I went inside while those other two stood guard for me and I just sat there and didn't touch her. I told her not to be afraid, that I wasn't going to hurt her. I can still see her face, the look on it, she was crying real soft but staring up at me all confused, like, 'What are you doing?' I waited maybe five minutes and went out, pretending to be hitching up my pants. Harris took out a wad of piastres from his pocket, money leftover from our resupply trip, wrapped in a rubber band, and he dropped it in her lap. And she took it. I knew what Harris was thinking—just in case we got found out, he could say she was a whore and that we'd paid her."

Marion's uncomprehending expression had not changed. Her mouth half open, she blinked rapidly, the way people do after a flashlight has been shined into their eyes. Fellowes could tell that she regretted, to the depths of her heart, insisting that she hear what he'd warned her not to hear.

"I take it you didn't report them," she began, paused, and went on, quietly but caustically. "You didn't snitch?"

"No."

"Because you were their lookout? Did you think that because you didn't. . ." She hesitated, her eyes skidding off his face. "Because you didn't actually *do it*, that that got you off the moral hook?"

"I was ashamed," he replied, shaking his head. "I was ashamed then, I'm ashamed now. I saw the brigade chaplain first chance I got and I went to confession, but that didn't make me feel any less ashamed."

"I wouldn't think so. Some priest's holy babble wasn't going to make it all right, just like your buddy giving her money wasn't going to make it any less than what it was. Maybe you yourself didn't touch that poor creature, but you did your bit."

Fellowes jumped up suddenly, as though from the action of a powerful spring, and threw his arms out wide, flung them back and forth, seeming to swat at invisible gnats.

"Do you suppose I don't know that? Do you suppose I haven't lived with it for . . . Sometimes I think about Keane and Paige and the others who never made it home alive, and I ask myself, 'Why did I survive? Why did Harris and Mackey?' Keane and Paige, they were better men than us.

They were more deserving. But it's come to me that being deserving didn't count. The war didn't discriminate, it killed bad men and it killed good men and men in between. Let me tell you where the deserving comes in—it's what you do with your life afterward. And I've tried to live my life like I was worthy of keeping it. I've tried to be a decent human being, a decent husband, a decent father. In all the time we've been married, I've never even flirted with another woman and I've worked hard and. . ."

Exhausted by this impassioned defense, and unsure where he was going with it, he dropped his arms to his sides and stopped speaking.

"No one is going to argue that you haven't been a good husband, a good father," she said. "Least of all, me. It's just that. . ."

"Just what? That there's no excuse for what I did? Damn straight there isn't." Revealing his secret history had taken Fellowes to such an emotional pitch that he was ready to bring about the thing he feared most. "All right, you wanted to hear it, you've heard it. Heard it all. If you don't think you can live with it, or live with me, then you can. . ."

Marion clasped his wrist and cut him off mid-sentence. "No melodrama, please, Tim. I was going to say that I just need time to process all this."

Fellowes began his trek up Núi Chúa the following morning. The road climbed in tight, torturous switchbacks; the sun struck ferocious blows. During the summer vacation between his sophomore and junior years, Father Phelan, his high school algebra teacher, had walked the Way of Saint James in Spain, all five hundred miles of it. The last leg, he'd told the class, had been on the Camino Primitivo, the ancient route trod by medieval pilgrims, many of whom sought expiation for their sins. The priest hadn't said if that was his reason for making the pilgrimage, but Fellowes thought of his own hike in those terms.

Marion was in the van with Jenter and Tráng, still "processing" everything she'd heard from him the previous afternoon. An awful lot to process. It was as if he'd stripped himself bare and shown her a repulsive chancre, previously hidden. The image of what he'd done must be branded on her mind. What would she do? He wouldn't blame her if she found it impossible to stay married to him. She was distant at last night's dinner hosted by the village chairman, and distant this morning, speaking scarcely a word to him, to anyone.

Two and a half hours into the climb, he rounded a sharp bend, beyond which the road ran level across the face of the mountain. He stopped to rest, guzzled from a water bottle in his backpack, and checked the GPS hung by a lanyard around his neck. Elevation: 748 meters. Multiply by 3.28 = 2,453 feet. Distance overall: 6.5 kilometers. Multiply by 0.621 = 4.03 miles. Damn. Not yet halfway. He wiped his face with a hand towel tied to his belt and walked on, the slopes on both sides extremely steep and forested by tropical oak and teak and mahogany trees. Far below lay a quilt work of tea plantations, rice paddies, and cane fields, cut here and there by slow, brown rivers. The country's beauty, like its birdlife, was something he'd barely noticed during the war.

He'd met the enemy at the chairman's dinner last night: two men around his age who had fought with the Viet Cong and who looked like twins. Both had leathery faces, shocks of white hair, and a serenity that Fellowes envied. Maybe it helped that they'd been on the winning side. The war did not obsess them, as it did him; the past did not cling to them, as it did him. Their attention was on the present and the future—building a new school for the district's children; fixing up the roads between villages. The war's absurdity struck Fellowes as never before. He was eating pork and rice and conversing with men he at one time would have done his best to kill, as they would have done their best to kill him.

Climbing further, he passed a road grader, construction and maintenance gangs swinging picks. A refreshing breeze blew down from the summit, the temperature dropped twenty degrees. He came to a gate with a sign announcing in Vietnamese, English, and French the entrance to

Núi Chúa National Park. An old rock-walled hill station, renovated into an inn and teahouse, stood to one side of the gate. He sat down on the terrace, ordered a bowl of pho from a lovely girl in a blue áo *dài,* and waited for the van to arrive from below. A light drizzle, more mist than rain, fell for ten minutes; then the van pulled up. Marion, in the back seat on the driver's side, lowered the window and raised a hand in greeting.

"Hi, hon. Pleased to see you haven't collapsed."

The term of affection encouraged him for a moment, but the expression in her gray-blue eyes, like a jeweler's assessing a diamond's worth, suggested that she'd spoken it out of habit.

"Hop in," said Jenter. "You've proved whatever it is you need to prove."

"I'm not trying to prove anything. I'll hump the rest of the way, thanks."

"Tim! Please get in," Marion pleaded. "You're sixty-six, for God's sake."

Her concern for his welfare also may have been habitual, he couldn't tell. Tráng warned, not entirely in jest, that tigers prowled the mountain, better be careful; but Fellowes's stubborn determination won out. Tráng opened the gate, the van went on ahead, and he resumed his pilgrimage.

He soon questioned his judgment. The grade grew steeper, the road turned to a yellowish clay, slick as ice. His calf muscles quivered from the strain. Cicadas sang, their high note a piercing screech that he could feel as well as hear. A part of him delighted in the self-imposed agony. Might there be redemption in it, might it cleanse the taint from his soul, and allow him to renew his friendship with himself? He trudged past another construction crew, too hard at work to notice him. Ten or fifteen minutes farther on, off to the right side, the first ruin appeared—a roofless villa wreathed in vaporous ribbons. Bullets and shrapnel from some forgotten battle scarred its crumbling stone walls. Another showed itself, then another and another, then two fragmented pillars blemished by mildew, vines twined around them like decorations. The mythical resort. It looked as if it were a thousand years old rather than less than a century.

The road leveled off again. He followed it through a grove of pine trees, or what looked like pine trees, and reached the summit. Elevation 1,619 meters = 5,312 feet. He was greeted by a sight so incongruous that he would have thought it a hallucination if he'd been on drugs: a restaurant, a terrace with plastic tables and chairs under festive umbrellas advertising Tiger and "33" beer, and four large dwellings with steeply-pitched tile roofs that were supposed to resemble Montagnard long houses but looked more like Swiss chalets. The van was parked beside a large sign that read, in the same three languages as the one below, WELCOME TO NUI CHUA RESORT. Marion, Jenter, and Tráng, seated at one of the tables, applauded as he crossed the terrace and flopped into a chair, trembling from exhaustion. His shirt looked as if he'd been swimming in it. He shivered as it and his skin dried in the cool air. He asked for a beer. Someone brought him a bottle of Tiger. Tráng gave him congratulatory pats on the shoulder.

"It is said that climbing this mountain on foot will tell you who you are."

And who am I? Fellowes thought.

The resort director, a moon-faced young man named Chinh, took them on a tour of the ruins in the afternoon. He carried a photocopy of a map or chart from 1933 with little squares showing the locations of the original bungalows and the owners' names printed below. The Ministry of Tourism, he said with a promotional flourish, planned to rebuild them and sell them to businessmen in places like Singapore and Hong Kong. It was to be a kind of condo development in the jungle, with a clubhouse, a swimming pool, a fitness center. Jenter, waving an arm at the rubble heaps, observed that the Ministry had its work cut out for it.

They traipsed after Chinh into one of the wrecked bungalows, where he grasped an iron ring in the floor, raised a trap door, and, shining a flashlight into the dark opening, reached inside and retrieved an intact bottle. The label was still legible, a Bordeaux, vintage 1927.

"A wine cellar!" Marion exclaimed.

"Not a true cellar, a storage place," said Chinh. "The wine has survived war and almost ninety years, and well-aged, ha-ha." He pointed at the chart. "It belonged to these people, Monsieur and Madame Paul Joubert."

Fellowes shuddered in a chilly breeze that seemed to have blown in from another climate zone. He shut his eyes, and this time the mental mechanism that usually took him no further back than 1970 transported him into a past beyond his own. His imagination instantly rebuilt the bungalow; he pictured the Jouberts, Monsieur wearing a tropical linen jacket, Madame a muslin dress, a houseboy in silk brocade pouring the wine. The vision, which lasted no more than two or three seconds, was as extraordinary as it was brief.

Chinh replaced the bottle, as if it were an invaluable artifact, and motioned for everyone to continue following him. The next attraction was a rubble field of considerable size: shattered timbers strewn like driftwood on dunes of brick and concrete—the remains of a twenty-room hotel for vacationing colonials who couldn't afford a villa or who were guests of the residents. An American bomb had struck it in 1972, said the director, stressing the projectile's nationality.

"A very big bomb, you can see the crater, I will show it to. . ."

He interrupted himself at the same time that Tráng called out, "*Con Trăn*!" and hopped backwards, bumping into Marion. Chinh also retreated, pointing at what Fellowes very briefly mistook for a fallen vine until it moved, ever so slowly, over a pile of debris.

"Good God, it must be twenty feet long," Marion said, staring in fascination. "What is it?"

"*Con Trăn*," Tráng repeated with barely contained terror.

"A python," Jenter translated. "Reticulated python. Longest snake in the world."

"And a *ma quī*, Jenter. A demon."

Chinh, with a *tsk* and a twitch of his head, dismissed his friend's superstitiousness. "We will look at the crater another time, for now tour is ended," he said, softly clapping his hands. "Let us have some drinks."

While the others filed off, Fellowes hesitated, mesmerized by the snake, the size of it, the beauty of its geometric markings, tan ovoids rimmed in black, triangles rimmed in yellow, the sinuous ripples in its body as it slithered over the mounded bricks and rock. Marion called to him, but something held him, some captivation he had no name for; and in the moment before the python slipped from sight, its tail rose and wiggled, and he had a sensation that it was beckoning him to follow. Christ, was he becoming as weird as Tráng? He, an electrical engineer who once designed guidance systems? A demon, Tráng had said. The devil is a serpent—a venerable idea and maybe not all that weird.

Marion came up and tugged him by the sleeve. "Tim, come on."

"I write poetry because the people you have seen, the farmers, the villagers, the workers on the road to this mountain, they do not know how to dream."

Tráng was speaking in the cavernous restaurant, where those same workers were eating at the long tables, like tables in a school cafeteria. The director, Chinh, was sitting next to him, and next to Chinh, the restaurant manager, a middle-aged woman named Li. Dinner was over, and a feast it had been: chicken and rice and cooked greens like okra, eggplant, fried onion, hard-boiled eggs. Marion and Fellowes had pretended to eat the appetizer—chicken claws arrayed in glasses like flowers in a vase. Jenter tore into them with relish, scraping off the thin, stringy meat with his teeth.

"How do you mean, they don't know how to dream?" Marion asked, squinting at Tráng.

"They have no dreams except to have enough clothes, enough rice to see them through to the next harvest. In those villages, the saying is, 'Pray for three bowls of rice a day and three shirts in the winter.' I try to show people how to dream for better. That should be the mission of all our poets. May I read you one of my poems?"

She nodded. Tráng picked up a paperback book, and with deep feeling recited slowly to allow Chinh time to translate. The poem was short and about birds flying over a graveyard, singing for the souls of the dead. The visit to the village cemetery two days ago had inspired it, Tráng said when he was finished.

"Uh . . . excuse me," said Marion. "But how would that show anyone how to dream? It's rather sad."

"Oh, yes. Do you know of the *Tale of Kiều*? Our greatest poem, written long ago."

He looked sidelong at Li, said something to her, and she began to sing in a high, haunting voice. She sang for two or three minutes before ending on an abrupt note, seeming to stop herself in mid verse. The lyrics were lines from the *Tale of Kiều*, Tráng said, then rendered the lines into English:

A prisoner now she must remain,
Locked in the Blue Pavilion and alone
In her young beauty. Only the distant mountains,
Though so far, she felt as friends, and the near moon
Watched at her window. . .

"Poor Kiều, her family in big money trouble," Li explained. "She is tricked into a prostitution house to save them."

There was a momentary silence before Marion threw up her hands and said, "My God, that's sad, too. Is all your country's poetry so sad?"

"War by war, death by death, storm by storm, this is a sad country, so our poetry must be sad," Tráng answered. He paused, raising his eyes toward a gigantic brown moth—it was as big as a bat—flitting around a light in the vaulted ceiling. Then he lit a cigarette, clamped it between his teeth, and gave Fellowes a long, searching look. "Tell me tomorrow what you dream about tonight."

After dinner, Fellowes and Marion sat talking on the small wood deck outside their room, which was in one of the imitation longhouses. Their chairs were side by side, and he leaned back in his, his left arm dangling in the gap between them: a silent plea for her to reach across and take his hand. But she was holding a guidebook, reading it by penlight. Tomorrow would begin a week of more traditional tourism, two days in Danang, two more in Hué, the remainder in Hanoi before flying home.

"It says here that the Temple of Literature in Hanoi goes back to the tenth century. There are stele engraved with the names of the scholars who received doctoral degrees. Can you imagine?"

"Imagine what?" he asked brusquely.

"Why, they're like . . . yearbooks. Stone yearbooks."

Fellowes gazed across a swath of blackness twenty miles wide at the lights of Danang jeweling Tourane Bay. He said nothing. Marion habitually pigeonholed her thoughts, her opinions, her emotions, a trait that sometimes irritated him. He supposed it had developed out of a lifetime of placing plants and animals in neat categories. Listening to her, you would never suspect that she'd learned something deeply upsetting about her husband only yesterday. That didn't mean she'd come to terms with her troubling new knowledge; no, she'd filed it away, to be retrieved when the time was right.

"We never knew that these people come from such an ancient culture. They were awarding doctorates way, way before America was even a gleam in Columbus's eye," she went on. "That woman . . . Li? Reciting the poem? Picture an American restaurant manager reciting Shakespeare to his customers."

"Goddamnit, Marion. . ."

"What?"

"Stop. Just stop. Stop acting and talking like everything is the same between us."

She lay the book in her lap and shut the penlight off. "I'm only trying to be pleasant. I'd like the next week to go pleasantly, that's all."

"Well, I'd like to know when and if you'll be done with your processing. I'd like . . . I *need* to know where I stand with you."

"It's not something we can deal with now. I don't want us to quarrel in front of Jenter and Tráng and whoever else might be around."

"Who's quarreling? I'm not going to argue that what I did back then was. . ."

She leaned toward him, raising her hand. "I meant it's too personal. Quarrel was the wrong word. And maybe processing was, too. Absorb might be better. I need time to fit the man I've loved and been married to since I was twenty-seven . . . I need to fit him in with the picture of him guarding his two buddies while they . . . And then going into that shed so they would think he was joining them in the crime, and not telling anyone what they did because he was afraid of them. I know that he wasn't much more than a kid, and that he'd seen things no nineteen-year-old should see, and that things had happened to him that shouldn't happen to anyone, and I know that isn't who or what he is now. But still . . . I'm a woman, and I cannot help but put myself in her place, imagining two big guys armed to the teeth, dragging me into a shed. . . . Oh, Tim, can't you see that merging the then-you with the now-you isn't something I can do overnight?"

Fellowes was again silent. *Climbing this mountain on foot will tell you who you are.* It had told him who and what he once was, an accomplice. Perhaps he, too, was trying to merge the then-him with the now-him.

"But I want you to know," Marion said, "that I do love you." And she reached out and took his hand, holding it lightly, almost indifferently; but she had taken it.

Chinh came for him in the morning, insisting that he show him the crater made by the American bomb. Marion and Jenter did not join them, for some reason. They walked through the grove of pines into the ruins, Chinh painting a picture of how the bungalows would look when they were rebuilt, a picture so vivid that Fellowes could see the red tile roofs restored, the walls all repaired and freshly painted. They passed the Joubert's villa, and he looked in and saw them as well, Monsieur in a jacket of tropical linen, Madame wearing her muslin dress, pearls sparkling on her elegant throat. They nodded to him, they said "bonjour," and invited him in for a glass of wine. He was about to accept when Chinh shook his head and with his fingers waved to him to keep walking. Soon, they were in front of the hotel, which had also risen from its wreckage and was filled with guests, more men in linen jackets or in cotton shirts open at the neck, and their ladies strolling about, semi-sheer dresses swirling around their ankles. Suddenly, in a tremendous explosion, the entire edifice was blasted into fragments, and Fellowes was standing with Chinh on the lip of a smoking crater that looked like a crater on the moon. "Go and see, see what your people have done," Chinh commanded, and Fellowes, as if in a trance, went down, slipping in a loose shale of pulverized brick and concrete. He did not see the python for the dense smoke. It materialized seemingly out of the smoke and struck with shocking speed, clamped its jaws around his right arm, then coiled its powerful body around his legs, his waist, his chest, throttling the air from his lungs. With a strength he didn't know he possessed, he seized the snake by its throat with his free hand and twisted so that its blunt-nosed head was facing him, and he was staring into its pearlescent eyes, dead as stones. He twisted again and again, freed his trapped arm, wrestled the python, a fight to the death until, with a loud cry and a single, mighty heave, he broke its grip. . .

"Tim! Tim! Wake up!"

His eyes opened. It was still dark, four in the morning. His mouth was dry as sand, his forehead slick with clammy sweat, his arm muscles twitching. Sitting up, he saw that the bedsheets were tightly wound, as if to form a makeshift rope, and were wrapped around him from the chest down.

"Bad dream," he murmured.

"I'll say. You yelled like bloody murder."

"I'm all right. Just a bad dream. Go back to sleep."

He stood with Tráng in the incandescent dawn, gazing westward at the Truong Son range, rolling away toward Laos. The dense mists in the ravines and gorges looked like vaporous lakes.

"You asked me to tell you what I dreamed last night," Fellowes said.

"Yes?"

He described the nightmare, which he recalled with amazing clarity. Tráng nodded but said nothing.

They packed their things, gave their thanks to Chinh and Ms. Li, and rode down the mountain and across the broiling lowlands toward Danang. Some two hours later, Pham pulled up to the entrance of the Hyatt Regency on what used to be called China Beach but now had some other name. He unloaded their luggage, and the bellhops carried it into the lobby. As Fellowes approached the front desk to check in, Tráng took him aside for a moment.

"I have been thinking about your dream," he said.

"Yes?'

"The python was the past. It was choking you. By coming here, you have freed yourself from its hold."

Fellowes considered this interpretation and glanced over at Marion, waiting for him at the desk alongside Jenter.

"That's a good thought," he said. "We'll see."

THE TRAVELER

Helen Coyne adored the aggressively antique décor in the *Jihan's* staterooms and salons. Cradle telephones with horn-shaped handsets, light fixtures with fluted mantles, teak-paneled walls summoned her grandmother's time, an age more graceful, stylish, and elegant than the vulgar, yawpish present. Her husband, Patrick, wasn't so enamored. He felt as if he and his fellow passengers—forty altogether, not counting the tour guides—were aboard a floating stage set, or better yet, a bubble insulated from the sweltering villages and cities into which they disembarked for brief sorties to temples, to markets peddling trinkets at inflated prices, to demonstrations of traditional crafts like making rice paper. Patrick regarded himself as a thoroughly practical man grounded in the world as it is, not as it used to be or as some wished it to be.

He and Helen had been to the Galapagos and Antarctica; this trip, a ten-day voyage up the Mekong River to the ruins of Angkor Wat, was the third they had booked with Greerson Expeditions, which catered to well-heeled clients who fancied themselves as adventurers exploring remote places that less privileged travelers—i.e. tourists—seldom saw. Patrick had been a foreign service officer for thirty-five years; he'd seen the world, had had his share of adventures, and knew that sailing on a ship tricked out to look like a relic from the early twentieth century was not one. It was a cruise and her passengers were tourists, unremarkable except for their money.

Helen was Patrick's second wife. His previous spouse, sick of pulling up stakes every two or three years to follow him from one posting to another, had left him midway through his career. Helen had been stuck in a drab marriage and a dead-end job marketing outdoor clothing and was relieved, even happy, when her husband did her a favor by dying at fifty-six. She married Patrick five years later, after he'd returned to the states from his final assignment in Iraq. His tales of far-off, dangerous lands enthralled her. She found him exciting and was consequently disappointed when he retired and settled down in Kent, Connecticut, declaring that he would not mind it at all if he never saw another suitcase, much less packed one. Signing up with Greerson Expeditions had been Helen's idea. Maybe he did not need new experiences in new places, but she did.

The impulse to jump ship struck Patrick the day the *Jihan* crossed into Cambodia, a country he'd been assigned to at the beginning of his career. The ship was moored to a dock in a border kampong while the authorities checked everyone's papers. Fishing boats swarmed the river, all manned by Vietnamese who had migrated, illegally, into Cambodia. Their presence greatly offended one of the local guides. He launched into a tirade damning the Vietnamese as "colonialists" who were corrupting his country's culture. The tour director, an American named Wilson, whisked him away and announced that after lunch the passengers were to go on an oxcart ride to visit a school and a pagoda.

Ten of these conveyances were lined up on the dock, like taxis at an airport or train station. A couple in their thirties or early forties, Paul and Tracy, joined Helen and Patrick in their cart. The slow, jarring ride through rice paddies and lotus fields put Patrick in a grumpy mood. Why did they have to travel this way in the twenty-first century? He was often grumpy these days, a "crabbed old fart" in Helen's words. He blamed this condition on the heart surgery he'd undergone about a year ago for atrial fibrillation and a blocked coronary artery. The operation had left him depressed for a long while, then depression curdled into irritability. Paul, an Oklahoman who traded commodity futures, and his wife weren't helping, both young and good looking and rich enough to have made a vocation of traveling to exotic destinations. The Himalayas. The Masai-Mara. The Amazon. They would not shut up about their journeys. The most recent had been a motorized dugout trip up the Sepik River in New Guinea to spend a couple of days and nights with a tribe of headhunters. The natives had stopped decapitating people in favor of hosting tourists, as the handsome couple, in full possession of their heads, proved.

"Still and all, it must have been scary," said Helen.

Paul gave a shrug that communicated a double-barrel answer: Some in their group thought it scary; they did not.

"But we did have one tense moment when the chieftain told Paul he wanted to spend the night with me," Tracy offered.

"No! Really?" said Helen. "How did you get out of that? . . . You did, didn't you?"

Paul replied that he'd referred the chief's request—it was almost a demand—to the tour group leader, who took the man aside and convinced him that screwing a guest would blacklist him and his people. No more tourist dollars.

What crap, Patrick thought. The couple's account encapsulated what he loathed about these so-called expeditions: their inauthenticity. The tour guide arrives to rescue the damsel from a bonking by the head headhunter, who probably had never split anything with his machete beyond a coconut. Paul and Tracy were dilettantes, like everyone on board, spending thousands to amuse themselves with make-believe experiences. They might as well don virtual reality headsets. He decided right then that he must get away, at least for a while. He might have jumped out of the jouncing oxcart if it had not been for his cellphone, vibrating in his back pocket,the one-thirty alarm reminding him to take his daily beta-blocker and blood thinner.

His chance came the next day, when the ship docked in Siem Reap and its passengers were herded into tour buses that shuttled them to a five-star hotel. Their guide told them they had the day free; tomorrow, they would visit Angkor Wat.

In his and Helen's suite, Patrick changed into tennis shoes, shorts, and a cotton shirt and declared he was going for a walk.

"Now? It's the heat of the day," she said. "A gajillion degrees."

"I'll stick to the sub-gajillion shade."

"You saw the lovely pool they have here. I'd rather go for a swim. Do you mind if I stay here?"

He did not mind in the least. In fact, he'd hoped she'd say that.

"Got your meds?"

He kept them in a contact lens case, which he plucked from a side pocket and shook it so she could hear the pills rattle.

Patrick hailed one of the tuk-tuks parked near the hotel entrance and settled into the seat. The driver, a slender young man with a smooth brown face that wore a ready grin and sunglasses, was named Wang.

"Where do you go?" he asked.

"Nowhere in particular. Wherever you want."

Wang gave his hourly rate. Patrick dug several large-denomination riels from his wallet and passed them to the driver and said, "That should cover it." His grin widening, brightening—he'd hit the jackpot—Wang pulled into traffic. The Central Market was the first stop on the improvised tour. Patrick strolled amid the stalls and bought a small decorative teak elephant. Then it was on to a restaurant, where he disembarked to eat blossom salad and skewered beef, then to a monastery on the Siem Reap River, where a monk showed him the Golden Buddha and the Reclining Buddha and various other Buddhas. Patrick took immense pleasure in the excursion, alone, away from his fellow travelers, away from Helen, whose enthusiasm often annoyed him. He was young and single again, or rather, he remembered, with a special vividness being young and single, a stranger in strange lands, meeting contacts in parks and bars and shadowy rooms. He'd been legendary for the information he'd mined from disgruntled civil servants, from opponents of whatever regime ruled whatever country he happened to be in. Even in this country he'd cultivated a source, and, as luck would have it, this source happened to be a very beautiful woman, and eventually his lover.

He left the monastery, and Wang inquired what Patrick would like to do next. "Do you wish to visit a temple?"

"Sure. But not if it's full of tourists."

"I know good temple place. The jungle temple. Like Indiana Jones. Very few go there."

"Perfect."

"But it is from here one hour. Higher price."

Patrick, begrudgingly admiring Wang's entrepreneurship, produced more bills and stuffed them into his driver's shirt pocket.

The trip took an hour and a half, the tuk-tuk put-putting down a rough road, slowed by creaking oxcarts and people on foot. Scenes not much different from those he recalled from the past. It was mid-afternoon when they arrived at the temple, and it did beg comparison with Indiana Jones's Temple of Doom: cracked walls caressed by tree roots so old they appeared to be part of the masonry; vines thick as a human calf choking broken pillars; piles of rubble. It delighted Patrick to no end that he was the only one there, except for a young woman seated on stool beside a ticket booth. She was reading a book.

"Jungle temple," said Wang with a swing of his arm, as if it were his creation. "There is my sister. She is guide."

"Your sister?"

"Yes. Very good guide. Her name Veasna. Very good guide. I will wait." Wang offered a wink. "No extra charge for waiting."

Veasna put down her book as Patrick approached and presented a welcoming smile. Her plain uniform—a white blouse with a name tag, khaki trousers—did not detract from her looks. A pale gold complexion, long black hair, black, captivating eyes. Patrick had no illusions about himself, his age apparent to all but the blind, so he figured that this enchanting beauty bestowed her smile only because she was bored and pleased to have someone to show around.

"Hi! Welcome to the Jungle Temple," she said almost without an accent. "My name is. . ."

Pointing to the tag pinned above her right breast, an ample breast, Patrick noticed.

"Yes, Veasna. Your brother told me."

"My brother?"

"Wang. The tuk-tuk driver who brought me here." Patrick made a half-turn to point him out and was baffled to find him gone. "He was here a minute ago. He must've gone off to park somewhere."

Veasna frowned. "I have no brother called Wang. No brother who drives tuk-tuk."

Patrick said nothing. Maybe he'd misunderstood Wang. Or maybe he'd meant "sister" as a metaphor. That wasn't all that baffled him: He'd seen Veasna before, he could swear it. But that was impossible; he hadn't been in this country in forty years, and she couldn't be older than twenty-five.

"Your broth . . . I mean, Wang said you could guide me around the temple."

She answered that she would be happy to, and after he paid the fee, stepped into the booth and gave him a ticket—an unnecessary formality considering that the place was deserted.

Overcoming his confusion about the missing Wang and the vague familiarity of Veasna's face, Patrick followed her through what must have been an entrance in some distant time but was now only two shattered pillars, one taller than the other, astride a dirt lane.

They scrambled over and around rubble, as she delivered a commentary on the temple's history: thought to have been built nearly a thousand years ago, during the reign of a king named Suryavarman; the inscriptions he saw on the walls were Hindu and Buddhist . . . Patrick half-listened, winded from clambering over huge stone blocks, heart beating faster than he liked; it threatened to start fibrillating. Twenty years ago, hell, ten, he would have done what he was doing now with ease. He asked Veasna if she had any water. She removed a squeeze bottle from her fanny pack and handed it to him. He drank greedily. It was as he passed the bottle back to her that something extraordinary happened: for an instant—no more than that—he saw Veasna in an olive-drab uniform, a checkered Khmer scarf wrapped around her throat. The woman who had been his source and lover and helped build his legend. God almighty, Veasna could be her double.

"Mister, you don't look well. Are you sick?"

"No . . . no . . . I'm okay." Patrick sucked in a breath. He stared at Veasna, his heart still thrumming. "It's just that you look like a woman I knew a long time ago. Chantary. Any chance you had a relative with that name? Your mother. . . . No, it would be your grandmother."

"Very sure. No brother called Wang, no grandmother called Chantary."

"A lovely name. In English, it means 'Beautiful Moon Girl,'" Patrick said. "May I ask you, if you know, what does Veasna mean?"

She squinted for a moment, then said, "Fate. Destiny. You are feeling better now? Shall we continue? I wish to show you the Central Sanctuary."

"Please."

The sanctuary was a temple within a temple. Its roof no longer existed, and liana vines wove a lattice overhead through which the sun poked fingers of light. It was refreshingly cool in the partial shadow. To Patrick, following Veasna as she interpreted the inscriptions etched into the ruined walls, the *Jihan* and its passengers and Helen seemed much farther away than a ninety-minute drive. He was a practical man who saw things as they were, yes, but he was not immune to indulging in fantasies now and then. He did indeed feel like Indiana Jones exploring the Temple of Doom.

He and Veasna walked through a dim passage and into a courtyard where the sunlight, after the shady interior, caused him to blink and see spots. When his eyes adjusted, he saw, across the courtyard, a stone staircase on the far side. It rose some thirty or forty feet out of a mound of broken brick and stone and ended in mid-air. Centuries ago, a tall tower stood there, Veasna said, and the staircase, three times its present height, led to its top. The tower represented Mount Meru, sacred to Hindus, Buddhists, and Jains alike.

"You see the platform at the top? From there you can see all the temple grounds. You would like to see?"

Patrick answered that he would.

The stairs, buttressed by the wooden framework that supported the viewing platform, were steeper than they'd appeared from a distance. He hadn't climbed more than ten or twelve before he had to pause to catch his breath. Then ten more, and ten after that to reach the platform. Gasping, he gazed out across the ruins, acres of them, blanketed by jungle canopy in some places, while in others crumbled structures showed through the holes in the mat of leaves, branches, vines. A creepy yet arresting sight. Exposed to the full force of the late afternoon sun, Patrick began to sweat freely; it dripped from his half-bald skull into his eyes, blurring his vision. Without warning, his heart flipped into a wild race and slowed to several irregular beats before it raced again. Goddamnit! AFib. He asked Veasna for her water bottle. Holding it in one hand, he reached with the other into a side pocket of his shorts for the contact lens case containing the beta-blocker. It wasn't there! Nor in the opposite pocket, nor in the back pocket where he kept his wallet. Nor in his shirt pocket, which contained only the carved elephant figurine. He must have lost the case. But where? When? Panic gripped him and heightened the arrhythmia, which deepened his panic, which heightened the arrhythmia further. . . . An acute pain bolted through his chest, shot into his head. The joints in his legs seemed to pop like rubber bands under too great a strain. Dizzy, he grabbed the platform's rail to stop himself from falling.

Veasna cried out, "Mister! Mister!" She sounded far away.

Then, to his relief, to his joy, he felt it, the lens case. It was in his shirt pocket after all. Quickly, before he lost all motor control, he opened one of the two caps, placed the beta-blocker on his tongue, and washed it down with a squeeze on the water bottle. The episode ended almost as suddenly as it had come on. He'd never known the medication to work so swiftly, so thoroughly. All normal in a matter of seconds. All good.

"Mister, we will return now," Veasna said softly. She wiped his damp forehead with her palm, her skin cool against his. "I think this climb too much for you."

Patrick had no awareness of descending the stairs, no awareness of walking back to the entrance. It was as if he'd been teletransported, like Captain Kirk in *Star Trek*. Wang was waiting for him at the ticket booth in the sputtering tuk-tuk. He said he was reluctant to make the drive back to Siem Reap because his headlight wasn't working properly and darkness would fall before they were halfway there.

"My village is nearby," Veasna said. "You can stay with me until morning."

She got into the passenger seat, and with a seductive flip of her chin invited Patrick to sit beside her, which he did, leaving a discreet distance between them.

He should call Helen, tell her he would be delayed overnight (making up some plausible excuse). But there was no cell service in this rural area, and besides, he didn't know the hotel's phone number.

Patrick asked Veasna if she knew the number and if she had a landline phone at her place, explaining why he wanted one.

"Do not worry. Your wife will be fine," she said, clasping his hand, threading her fingers through his. Her touch was as comforting as it was erotic. For no good reason he could think of, he accepted the reassurance as if it were an irrefutable prophecy. Helen would be fine while he embarked on an adventure like none he'd experienced since he was young. The legendary Patrick Coyne. Coyne of the Realm, the station chief had nicknamed him for the intel he brought back from his liaisons with Chantary.

Wang started off, without asking Veasna for directions. Apparently, he knew the way. Soon, in deep twilight, he left the highway and went up a dirt road and stopped in front of a pond in whose still waters lotus flowers floated like small, pink boats. Patrick could just make out a white-walled compound a short distance away. Veasna got out of the tuk-tuk and, beckoning him to follow, began to walk toward the compound on a path beside a shallow stream that flowed into the pond. Again, she took his hand. Patrick breathed in the blossoms' fragrance, and their scent awakened an awareness that he didn't care if Helen would be fine. He didn't care, much to his amazement, if he never saw her or home again. A full moon was out. It illuminated bas reliefs carved into the stream's sandstone bottom: Brahma, the Creator, reclining on a serpent in the Ocean of Milk. A lotus flower sprang from Brahma's navel and on it rode Vishnu, the Sustainer. How did he, Patrick, know that without instruction from his guide? In the next moment, stopping in his tracks, he answered his own question.

"I recognize this place! I've been here before!"

Chantary—that's who she was, Chantary resurrected—looked up at him.

"Congratulations. It took you long enough to remember. I brought you here. Come."

She tightened her grip, gave him a tug, and continued toward the compound, its walls as white as the moonlight. A tall, stone sculpture of a male figure seated with legs crossed in the lotus position and a trident in one hand stood alongside the solid wood entrance gate. A cobra was coiled around his throat, its hood flared in venomous menace. Patrick froze in his tracks.

"Shiva," he whispered. "Lord Shiva. The Destroyer."

"You are afraid?" Chantary asked.

"Yes."

"But you know you should not be. Lord Shiva is much more than the Destroyer. You do not remember?"

Patrick thought for a few moments, thought and stared at the cobra's ruby eyes.

Chantary gave him a hint. "You see the snake's coils are three. Why is that?"

"They're symbols. Past, present, future all one thing. Lord Shiva is indifferent to time."

"And to what else"

"Death. He's indifferent to time and death."

"Come, then, Patrick. We will go inside. There is nothing to fear. . ."

Reynolds, the ship's doctor, sat in the hotel bar with the tour director, Wilson. Each was drinking a double scotch, straight up.

"How is she?" Wilson asked.

"As together as anyone could be under the circumstances. We got her on the plane alright."

"Probably in shock. I might be myself. We've never had anything like this happen before. What do you think . . . I mean, how do you think he died?"

"He had a stroke, you ask me," Reynolds replied. "But I think the fall was what did it. Those stairs are pure stone. The hospital doctor said Coyne had one helluva gash in his head. I didn't see it, so I can't say for sure, but it makes sense that he had a stroke, lost his balance, and tumbled down the stairs."

They were silent for a while, sipping their whiskeys.

"A guy his age . . . probably shouldn't have been traipsing around in the boondocks, all by himself," Wilson said. "What makes you think he had a stroke?"

"His wife told me he had AFib, atrial fibrillation. That can cause a stroke. And the woman who was guiding him said he grabbed his head and groaned and reached for a railing to steady himself. Next thing she knew, he staggered and went down those stairs."

"Helluva thing," said Wilson.

"Y'know, he wasn't dead when he landed. Still breathing, and even tried to say something. Or so I was told."

"Said what?"

"Something about the Moon. Babble. It didn't mean anything."

EZRA'S DOOR. . .

. . . had been salvaged when the Hall sisters' boarding house was demolished in . . . well, the date of its demolition is uncertain; it was some time after Ezra Pound had become famous. The door was said to have been stored in the basement of a building on the Wabash College campus. No one knew which building. No one had seen it since its removal from the rubble. Langford, like Pound a poet, though one with a far more modest reputation, had been hired as the school's writer-in-residence for the fall term. He learned about the legendary door at a faculty get-acquainted dinner hosted by Sandra Heiss, chair of the English Department. It was a warm evening in late August, a week before classes started. Nine people, ten counting Langford, were seated at a long table on the outside deck of a restaurant overlooking Sugar Creek, a tributary of the Wabash River. The subject of the door came up when, to fill a gap in the conversation, he mentioned that he'd noticed, on a map of Crawfordsville, Indiana, that a racetrack called the Ben-Hur Speedway was located just outside town.

"How did it get that name?" he asked, picturing Charlton Heston whipping a team of horses. "I assume they don't race chariots."

"Nope. Go-Karts," The answer came from Avery Sforza, professor emeritus, a man with multiple chins that created a chinless effect, his face merging into his neck in a smooth blend of flab. "It's Indiana's premier dirt track."

"That's why it's called the Ben-Hur Speedway?"

"Lew Wallace. He was Crawfordsville's famous son, a Civil War general. He wrote *Ben-Hur.*"

"And we have one other famous literary son," Heiss said. Tall, gray haired, rather severe looking in a dark suit—her appearance fit right in with Wabash's early history as a citadel of Presbyterianism—she looked at Langford as if he should know whom she was talking about. He did not confess his ignorance. He chewed on a piece of prime rib and nodded.

Heiss saw through the pretense and said: "Ezra Pound. Not truly a native son. He wasn't from Crawfordsville, but he taught at Wabash for not quite two semesters. *Not quite* because he was asked to leave."

"Fired. Bounced. Heave-hoed," Sforza added.

Then Heiss told the story of how the great poet, the creator of Imagism, the author of the epic *Cantos*, friend of Yeats, Eliot, Hemingway, etc., only twenty-three years old in the winter of 1908 and not yet great or even remotely famous, had been teaching Romance languages at the college, in whose Calvinist precincts he'd acquired a reputation for Bohemian flamboyance, wearing velvet jackets and Panama hats, throwing soirees for his students in his room at a boarding house owned by the staid sisters Ida and Belle Hall.

"A lot of drinking," she went on. "Wine, beer, Curacao when he could afford it."

"The guy was as out of place in Indiana as a toucan," Sforza interjected. "He called it 'the sixth circle of hell.'"

"But little Crawfordsville did have its diversions," Heiss said. "There were three vaudeville theaters in town. And starring in one of them was a British burlesque queen, a *transvestite* no less. . . . Shall I abbreviate?"

"Please."

Pound had befriended the actress the previous semester, Heiss related. One frigid night in February, he went to the train station to mail a letter to his parents in Philadelphia. And there he found the actress, huddled on a bench, alone, hungry, half-frozen. Her vaudeville troop had abandoned her, for reasons now lost to history. Taking pity on her, Pound brought her to his room, where she spent the night. He left for his classes the next morning. Later on, the sisters Hall went to the room to clean it, and discovered the young woman, the male impersonator, asleep in Ezra's bed.

"A major scandal in those times," Sforza said. He mashed some peas against the back of his fork. "Might even be one today, what with all the touchiness about sexual harassment. A prof pats a female on her arm— forget any other anatomical part— and he's a potential rapist."

"Avery, *please,*" Heiss said. She turned to Langford. "So, the Halls were close to the college president, a man named Macintosh. The women— they considered themselves moral guardians—reported the indiscretion to him, and—I'm really abbreviating now—Pound was let go. . ."

"Tell him about the door," Sforza said.

"The door, yes. A campus myth. The door to Pound's room. Some years after his departure, the boarding house was torn down, another building put up in its place. Someone, a maintenance man perhaps, salvaged the door, or so the legend has it, and stashed it in the cellar of a campus building. People have looked for it but never found it."

"A door?"

"It was gray and white."

"I mean, why the door?" Langford asked. "Why salvage a door?"

Heiss dabbed her lips with her napkin. "Well, Pound was given severance pay, and he used it to book passage to Europe. That's where he met Yates and Eliot and everyone else, wrote and published his early poems. So, you can say the door is an artifact because what went on behind it changed the course of modern literature."

"Better to say what the prudes *thought* had gone on behind it," Sforza said. "See, old Ezra never canoodled with the actress. He wasn't even in the room that night. He stayed somewhere else. When the board found that out, they met and reconsidered and told Pound he could stay on . . ."

"But he didn't," Heiss interjected. "He was so pissed off that he more or less told the Board where they could go. And off he went to Europe, and the rest, as they say, is history."

In the off-campus apartment provided for visiting lecturers, at a little past three the next morning, Langford woke enveloped in dread. He flopped an arm across the bed, half expecting to feel the reassuring warmth of his wife's body; then he remembered that he was eight hundred miles from New York, in a strange room in a strange town that would be his home for the next four months. Having delivered author talks and readings at universities and symposiums and literary festivals all over the country as well as twice in England, he was as accustomed to sleeping in beds not his own as a traveling salesman; strange surroundings had nothing to do with the cold terror that had startled him awake. He'd begun to experience spells of it several months ago, and it was as likely to strike in familiar places as not.

They came on at night, most often in the penumbral moments between consciousness and sleep; sometimes, like now, they woke him at a ghastly, post-midnight hour, his palms sweaty and tingling unpleasantly, his pulse racing as if he were on a treadmill, his whole system on high alert to meet some unspecified menace. Nothing could relieve these sensations, not reason nor will nor pills; but he had found that making note of each attack in writing often hastened its departure. It was a way of talking to himself.

He shuffled to the large walnut desk in the living room (the apartment was handsomely furnished), switched on the green-shaded desk lamp, and opened his daily journal, in which he scribbled:

> Aug.29, Three and change in the A.M. Another attack of the heebie-jeebies, the fantods, whatever the hell they can be called. A feeling that I'm on a ledge, about to lose control of myself, tumble into madness. Can't fathom why. Saw a shrink about them. He told me they're acute anxiety reactions, without saying what he thinks I'm anxious about. Assured me that as long as I'm afraid of losing my mind I'm not in fact losing it.

An academic distinction, Langford thought. He sat staring at the desk lamp for a few minutes, then went to the couch and began reading from a collection of Alice Munro's short stories. He was very much a Munro fanboy. Her prose, so simple and quiet, yet capable of sharp observations and striking images, usually calmed him when scribbling in his journal failed. But the magic wasn't working this time.

Beyond his journal entries and emails and the infrequent letter, Langford had been unable to write a word in more than two years. It was to ordinary writer's block as a five-mile traffic jam is to a long stoplight. Three years, eight months, and twenty-two days had passed since his last book, his third, had come out. Reviews had been spotty—most fell into the "failed promise" category—and sales dismal even by the standards for poetry collections. If it had not been for a part-time teaching gig at the New School, his income would have qualified him for welfare. Sondra's job, executive creative director at BBDO, brought in twice as much in a month as he did all year. She paid the mortgage on their condo; paid the utility bills and private-school tuition for their daughter; she put food on the table; and bought tickets to plays and movies when they needed a night out. He felt like a kept man, a situation he'd begun to find intolerable. A situation he was inclined to finger as the culprit behind the fantod hee-bie-jeebies, if for no other reason than it provided a concrete explanation.

Langford's first two books, a quirky memoir of his combat tour in Afghanistan, followed by a collection of (also quirky) poems, had earned favorable comparisons to James Dickey from reviewers. The hard-drinking former football player and World War II fighter pilot was Langford's literary hero. He wasn't a hard drinker himself—his alcoholic father had made him phobic about booze—but he was otherwise in the Dickey mold of the warrior-poet. Or had been. His early success had spoiled him. He'd committed the error of believing the praises critics threw at him, so that, when he began his third book, he couldn't recapture the unselfconscious state in which he'd written the first two, when it seemed as though he'd been taking dictation from some god occupying his own head.

The offer from Wabash had been unexpected; he'd accepted right away. The money wasn't much, but more than he earned at the New School. And he looked forward to time away from Sondra. She'd never complained about being the breadwinner, did not reproach him, even seemed proud to be married to a poet who'd won acclaim. He reproached himself, watching her leave for work before he sat down to struggle, unsuccessfully, to put something down on paper or on his laptop screen. Langford's poetry was considered cutting edge, but he was otherwise a traditionalist. A man worthy of the name ought to be able to support a family. His father had been a drunk, but a high-functioning drunk; he'd kept a roof over the heads of his family of five without Langford's mother contributing a dollar or a dime.

Still, that was not the sole reason, nor even the main reason he felt inadequate. His whole identity was bound up with his work; a writer unable to write was like a ballplayer who couldn't hit, field, or throw. He'd been something of a somebody; now he wasn't and was fading into irrelevance.

His thoughts flitted like insects, lighting on one topic after another; then, inexplicably at first, they settled on a memory of a trip he and Sondra had taken to Mexico, after visiting her retired parents in Arizona. Hundreds of pilgrims, on foot and horseback, were on the road south from the border to a festival in a town called Magdalena, where hundreds more crowded the main plaza or formed long lines filing into a white mission church: the chapel of San Francisco Javier, Magdalena's patron saint. Langford and Sondra went inside, where people shuffled past a life-size, wooden figure representing the saint lying on a coffin. It looked like a mannequin. Some people embraced the figure and lifted it by its head and shoulders and kissed its cheek. Some ran their hands down its chest, murmuring prayers. Or what Langford assumed were prayers. Sondra, who spoke good Spanish, asked a well-dressed woman what was going on. Some pilgrims were asking favors of San Francisco Javier, she answered, like pleading for a cure to a serious illness; some were fulfilling a mandate—a *manda*, she called it—to thank him for favors granted in the past year, say a crippled child who'd miraculously walked again.

The scene reeled in his mind, as clear and sharp as a video. In minutes, it did what reading Munro and writing in his journal had failed to do. The throbbing in his pulse faded, and with it the sense that a nameless but real disaster was about to befall him. He felt in command of himself once again, but he kept the light on and did not go back to bed or stretch out on the couch with his eyes shut. No point in inviting the fantods to have another go at him. He got up and went to the bathroom and peed and that was when he saw why the memory of that afternoon in Mexico had come to him.

"Can I ask why you're so fixated on that door?"

Avery Sforza spread his elbows on his desk and clasped his chubby hands to form a triangle.

"You said it the other day. What went on behind that door, or what people *thought* had gone on, changed the course of modern literature." Langford was in Sforza's office, on the second floor of Center Hall, a red brick Victorian that looked as if it had been relocated to the Midwest from New England. "It's an artifact. I'd like to see it."

Sforza did not see that he was lying, or, more accurately, speaking a half truth.

"So how do you think I can help you?"

"You said you're pretty sure the door was salvaged, that it's somewhere on campus, in a basement or storeroom."

"I am, yes." Sforza welded his thumbs together and stuck them under the slab of flesh that was once a chin. "You'll want to know why. Okay, when I first started teaching here—that was a while ago—I happened to be speaking with the head of the maintenance department, and he asked me who Ezra Pound was, and I told him, and he said he'd found a door in a pile of stuff in a basement. Wired to the door handle was a tag that had written on both sides, 'Door to Ezra Pound's room. Do not destroy or throw out.' So, someone at some time, probably right after his rooming house was torn down, had an idea pretty much like yours. It was a piece of literary history and he wanted to save it."

"But you don't know where this mystery man stored it?"

"Nope."

"You weren't curious?"

"Can't remember. It was thirty-five years ago, and I was new here. Had other things on my mind."

"So how did the story that a janitor junked it get started? You mentioned the other day that you didn't think that's what happened."

"Just a hunch. I think the mystery man—could've been a woman, got to be careful these days, y'know, DEI, diversity, equality, inclusion—I think he *or she* knew its value, historical value, I mean, and stashed it somewhere. Probably thought of selling it to a collector but never got the chance. . . . Wait a sec. . ." Sforza's hands parted. "I do remember that at one time the door had been in the college archives. Those are in the library. It must have been moved from there, so that's a good place to start your search."

Quest, Langford thought. *It's a quest, not a search.* Classes didn't start till the following week, he was all checked in with the English Department, he would have the time.

Sforza opened a drawer and handed Langford a booklet titled *Wabash College Campus Tour Guidebook*. "This will help you find your way around," he said.

Langford cut across the Mall to the Lilli Library, where he was directed to the archivist, Amy Wessel, a stout, elderly woman who presided over her domain from a tidy book-lined room, furnished with blond tables and chairs. He introduced himself, explained what he had come for, and was gratified when she did not ask why he was interested in a *door* but responded with an excited flash in her golden-brown eyes.

"I've often wondered myself what happened to it," she said in an open, cheerful voice. "We're mostly digitized these days, but we do keep physical artifacts. That for instance." She gestured at an easel in a far corner. It held a large, laminated poster advertising a football game between Wabash and Notre Dame in 1927. "That door was down here once upon a time."

"You don't know what happened to it?"

"I do not."

"There's a story that a janitor threw it out and it ended up in a landfill. Not enough room for it."

"We never have enough room."

"Some people don't believe it was tossed out."

"Maybe and maybe not. I looked for it many years ago, no luck. I do a blog, you know. A blog every month on some aspect or other of the school's history."

"Oh?"

"Yes, and it's a great deal of fun, and I did one on the occasion of Mr. Pound's"—she threaded her fingers and gazed toward the ceiling—"one hundred twenty-fifth birthday. October 30, 2010. Care to see it?"

Langford nodded, and Wessel turned to her desktop, tapped a few keys, then beckoned him to come round to her side of the table. There, on screen, was a page from the college magazine, edition of 1907, and on the page a faculty photograph of the young genius in profile. Skinny neck, hair neatly trimmed, a sharp nose slightly upturned. It looked like a police booking photo. Beneath it was a note that "Pounds" was the only faculty member not to face the camera, a brief biography, and an enigmatic comment: "Ezra Pounds should have been a blacksmith."

"Misspelled his name," Langford said.

"Yes. Sloppy proofreading. Read on."

Langford did, and fixed his eyes on a comment from an alumnus who also had become fascinated with Pound, though for different reasons: "*Good Presbyterians have standards of rectitude in financial matters as well as sexual ones. . . . Wabash had signed a contract with Mr. Pound to pay him a year's salary, and so they did."* Commenting on the comment, Wessel had blogged*: It was the Indiana college's generous—and probably unnecessary—payout that financed Pound's subsequent exploits in Italy's greener pastures.*

"That refers back to the incident of the woman discovered in his room," Wessel said. "The College paid him what was due, he used the money to sail to Europe, and. . ."

"The rest is history," Langford said.

"Yes. Yes, it is. Which brings us back to the door."

"Any suggestions where I might look for it?"

Little finger to her slender lips, three pressed to a cheek, she thought briefly.

"There are at least twenty-five buildings on this campus, and I think most have cellars or storage rooms. Could be any one of them, or it could have migrated to some place off campus by now. You'll need to contact Randall. Randall Mills, he's head of maintenance. He can let you in."

"Where do I find him?"

"In Center Hall. The basement level."

He took her hand, surprised by the strength in it, and thanked her.

"Let me know how it goes," she said. "Oh, by the way, tread carefully around Randall. He can be difficult."

Langford retraced his steps to Center Hall, took the stairs to the basement, and found Mills, a black man with a keg-like torso, wearing rimless glasses low on his nose, ensconced in a cramped cubicle, one wall of which was decorated with reports of some kind on clipboards aligned like parade-ground soldiers. He did prove to be difficult, demanding that Langford show him faculty ID, and after he'd done so, berating him for thinking that he, Mills, could designate one of his janitors to escort him around campus, opening up storage rooms for Langford's inspection. He had to deal with a problem in the heating system in one classroom building, a problem with toilets not flushing properly in a faculty lounge, and a dozen other things that needed to be fixed or looked at before classes started in just a few days.

"And you suppose that me or my people have got the time to help you look for an old door? A door, for Jesus's sake. A door that probably got thrown out way before I was a gleam in my daddy's eye. In all my years here, I never heard of such a thing."

"I was hoping," Langford, suitably chastised for his presumption, began, "that you might be able to. . ." His glance fell on a shelf, where he noticed a photograph of a much younger Mills in a uniform, sergeant's stripes on the sleeve. "Point me in the right direction, one old soldier to the other."

"I wasn't no goddamn soldier, I was a *marine,"* Mills said. "Now if you don't mind, sir, I've got things to do."

Feeling a bit ashamed as well as ridiculous, Langford hurried back to Wessel, told her about Mills's rebuff, and asked, with some diffidence, if she might intervene on his behalf.

"With Randall?"

"With whoever. I'm not planning to steal the damn thing," he said, shyness giving way to irritability.

"I'm not sure that would be . . . I might try to charm him, but . . . I am rather busy. . ." She motioned at two cardboard file boxes on an adjacent table. "Sorting through the papers of Ira McBride. He was the college president who engineered Pound's dismissal. Coincidence, I guess. Jealousy could have been involved. Do you know that story?"

Langford sighed as he shook his head.

"Before Pound took up residence at the rooming house on Washington Street—that's the one where the vaudeville girl was seen—he'd rented a room over on Meadow Avenue, and began flirting with a young widow, Mary Young, the landlord's sister-in-law. She was visiting. Well, guess what? President McBride was much taken with her, wanted to marry her, and I suppose Pound's attentions didn't sit well with him. Or with the landlord. He kicked Ezra out, and that's how he ended up at the Washington Street place. Interesting, don't you think?"

Langford wanted to say, *so what*? but kept silent.

"There's a rather ardent letter to Miss Young in one of these boxes," Wessel said, patting the covers of both. She tugged at a scarf around her neck, although the weather on this clear day in early September did not call for a scarf. "It looks like McBride never sent it. Very meticulous, the way he organized his papers. Know what I find fascinating about what I do?"

"No," Langford answered. Nor did he care. Again, he kept silent. It would be wise not to offend Ms. Wessel.

"You read through someone's letters, their diaries, their reports and written requests. You look at photographs of them at different ages. You see where they lived and who they were married to, if they were married, and articles about them and biographies, and in time that person *becomes alive* to you. You feel that you know them better than the people who did know them when they were living. You feel like you could talk to them. It's the nearest thing to time-travel I can imagine."

Langford nodded politely, and said after a few more seconds of silence, "Ah . . . you started to tell me that maybe you could speak to Mills? Put in a good word for me? Maybe you'd be able to convince him that I'm doing some research for you on the side. And finding the door. . ."

She reached across the table and warmly clasped his wrist. "I'll see what I can do."

She couldn't do much, or wouldn't. So it appeared. Classes began the following week. Langford had only two—a creative writing seminar with eight students, and a course in modern poetry, 1940–1990, with a dozen. All men. The school was one of a handful of single-sex schools remaining in the US. Preparing his lectures and delivering them took up around ten hours a week, occasionally a little more, leaving him plenty of time to work on his own stuff. But the blockage remained, as solid and immovable as a concrete wall. He called or emailed Sondra almost daily, avoiding complaints about his inability to write, and would feel empty afterward and sit and stare out his front window.

The leaves began to turn at the end of the month, and by early October the reds and golds and oranges shone in full splendor, reminding him of his time at Colby College in Maine. Langford never graduated, seized in the middle of his sophomore year by an intense restlessness, a fever that wouldn't break. He quit, and under the spell of Kerouac and the Beats, hitchhiked out West, then enlisted in the US Air Force, under the spell of his hero, Dickey. He never flew fighter planes; he was assigned as a crew member on a C5 cargo plane flying into and out of Bagram airfield. Taliban rocket and mortar attacks and suicide bombers struck often enough to earn Senior Airman Thomas Langford a Purple Heart (for what amounted to no worse than a deep cut in his left arm) and a Combat Action Ribbon. These incidents also gave him bad dreams for quite a while after he returned to civilian life, a minus compensated by the plus of providing material for his first book, *Fragments*.

One night in his apartment, his creative brain as blank as the sheet of paper on his desk, he mulled Wessel's description of fanciful resurrections, breathing life into persons long dead by reading their correspondence and diaries, by studying their photographs and biographies and what people had to say about them. *You almost feel you could talk to them, nearest thing to time travel you can imagine.* He had a volume of Pound's poetry in his library at home, phoned Sondra, and left a message to send it to him. Not the ebook version but the actual book. It arrived four days later, with a note—"Took me a while to find this. FedExed it in case you needed it right away. Love, S." He pressed the note to his nose. No scent of perfume, but he thought he could smell her regardless.

The college library provided the *Cantos* and a collection of Pound's letters and a biography by John Edwards. As the leaves reached peak, then browned and fell and bare branches groped like skeletal fingers at November's dull skies, Langford immersed himself in Pound: his early poems, his first Imagist verse, *In a Station at the Metro,* brief as a haiku—*The apparition of these faces in the crowd: Petals on a wet, black bough*—then *Hugh Selwyn Mauberley*—and selections from the *Cantos.* He looked at photos of Pound as a young man, with his piercing stare, and as a white-bearded old man, and listened to vintage recordings of Pound reading his works in a somewhat high voice and continental accent. He followed his life from his birth on the Idaho frontier in 1885, through his friendships in Europe with the great Modernists and his marriage to Dorothy Shakespear; his affair with his mistress, Olga Rudge; the births of his daughter and son; his seduction by Mussolini's fascists when he lived in Italy; his conviction for treason in 1945 and subsequent incarceration in a psychiatric ward—in lieu of a firing squad—and his final years in Venice, where he died in 1972, age eighty-seven. By Thanksgiving break, Langford felt he knew the man personally, much as Wessel had experienced with the subjects of her research.

He flew to New York for the holiday and was grateful for two things: 1. Sondra was horny, and 2. They did not have to host a turkey dinner for twelve—that task fell to her sister and brother-in-law in Connecticut. Returning to Crawfordsville the following week, he resumed what he now thought of as his daily Ezra bath. Not only did he feel he *could* talk to Pound, he did, making sure he did so silently and only when alone in the house.

Early the next month, on a wild, wintry night with freezing rain crackling against his windows—a night much like the one when Pound rescued the burlesque queen—the monologue became a dialogue: Pound spoke to him. Langford heard the poet's voice distinctly in his own head, asking "Why in hell are you so interested in me, what do you want?"

"To find the door to your room, the one in the rooming house on Washington Street," Langford replied, even as he wondered if he was losing his grip on reality. "If you want to know why. . ."

"I already know. It's your intention to run your hands over it, to embrace it, like those Mexicanos you saw hugging the statue of the saint. An icon with magical powers. You think if you do that, you'll cure your writer's block, you think it might even make you a genius."

Langford was shocked by the accuracy of this statement.

"I've two pieces of bad news for you," Pound said. "I've got no goddamn idea what became of that door, and number two, take a look at what I wrote for *T.P.'s Weekly*, edition of June 9, 1913."

"*T.P.'s Weekly*?" Langford said; he'd never heard of it.

There was no answer.

The next day, after his creative writing seminar, he went to see Amy Wessel. Was she familiar with a periodical called *T.P's Weekly*? Specifically, an edition from June 9, 1913? An article written by Pound? She was not, but was certain she could find it on the Web.

"It's twelve-thirty." she said, tapping her watch with a forefinger. "Why don't you go to lunch? I should have something for you by the time you're done."

When he came back, his gut churning from too much coffee and a mushy, faculty-lounge BLT, Wessel greeted him with a cheerful smile.

"It was June 6, 1913," she said, and waved at her desktop. "There was no edition of June 9. *T.P's Weekly* was a British literary journal in the early twentieth century. Pound was in London then. You could've found this yourself, you know. Just type the title in the search box, and there it is. I'll forward it to you right now."

After that was done, Langford asked if she would mind him reading it in her office. She motioned at an armchair tucked into a corner between two bookshelves. He sat down, opened his laptop, and clicked on the link to the forwarded message. The photocopy of a page dense with three columns of small type appeared on screen. Above the headline—"HOW I BEGAN— BY EZRA POUND"—was the date—June 6, 1913—followed by the publication's name. A brief chill, as from a cold breeze, passed through Langford. Had he actually communicated with Pound, and Pound with him? He must have. How else would he have known about this article if he'd never heard of *T.P.'s Weekly*? But why and how would Pound have given him the wrong date? If he wasn't losing his grip on reality, then . . . what? Then he'd had a conversation with a man who'd been dead since 1972. With a ghost! *The nearest thing to time travel I can imagine.* Could he have journeyed into the past? But that was impossible, wasn't it? Time's arrow always flew forward, didn't it?

Langford put these questions aside for the time being, zoomed the page, and began to read:

> *If the verb is put in the past tense there is very little to be said about this matter. The artist is always beginning. Any work of art which is not a beginning, an invention, a discovery, is of little worth. The very name Troubadour means a "finder," one who discovers . . .*

He came to the end, some two thousand words later, and, puzzled as to the reason he'd been directed to this essay, he read it again, seeking a clue. About midway through a paragraph caught his attention:

> *I knew at fifteen pretty much what I wanted to do. I believed that the "Impulse" is with the gods; that technique is a man's own responsibility. A man either is or is not a great poet, that is not within his control, it is the light from heaven, the "fire of the gods," or whatever you choose to call it. His recording instrument is in his own charge. It is his own fault if he does not become a good artist—even a flawless artist.*

Langford highlighted the paragraph and looked up at Wessel, who was thumbing through some document on her desk. "Hey, can I bother you a sec?" She nodded. He stood and set the laptop down in front of her. "How would you interpret the part I've highlighted?"

She read it and frowned and answered that Pound's meaning was rather obvious: talent, greatness, is inborn, like the color of one's hair or eyes; but it's the poet's responsibility to develop his gift through hard work and craftsmanship. Blame for failure to do so falls on him.

"But why would. . ." Langford stopped himself. He needed to phrase what he was about to say correctly, so she wouldn't think that he'd gone a bit off his rocker. "I'm going to tell you something I'd like to keep between us. Okay with you?"

She offered him a comic flicker of her eyebrows and said, "I love secrets."

He then recounted his experience on the previous night. "I'm not saying that I talked to him like I am with you right now," he added. "It was all in my mind or my imagination or something. But if I hadn't heard him mention '*T.P.'s Weekly*' how the hell would I have known there was such a magazine if I hadn't heard of it before? And the fact that he told me the wrong date, that sort of suggests he'd gotten mixed up in his own mind, meaning that I was . . . well, y'know . . . really having a conversation with him. I know it sounds goofy, worse than goofy. . ."

"I'm afraid it does," Wessel interrupted and cupped her hand over his and said in a maternal, my-dear-boy manner, "I can't explain this mystical encounter you had, and I promise not to say anything about it to anyone. But . . . if you don't mind a little unsolicited advice, It seems to me you're a little stressed out. Maybe you should forget this business about Pound and the door, stop reading him and thinking about him. . ."

Langford felt a flash of resentment, which he suppressed.

"Maybe I should put it this way," Wessel went on, her eyes fixed on him. They were a peculiar color, a butterscotch. "Let's say you were communing with Mr. Pound's spirit, a sort of seance. He was telling you to quit looking around for an old door and focus on honing your craft, your talent."

"Yeah. That's where most of the stress is coming from. I haven't been able to write a postcard for two years, and. . ."

"You've gotten it into your head that you need a magic bullet, or a magic door. Alright. Tell you what. I'll have another talk with Randall, I'll say that you're working on a research project for me and could he kindly cooperate."

Less than a week later, she phoned him at home. Randall had made copies of the keys to storage spaces he thought large enough to contain a door. There were seven altogether, a number Langford found auspicious. He was welcome to them, under the conditions that he was to lock up when he was through, not remove a single item, not so much as a paperclip or tool or box, and return the keys to Randall. Thrilled, anticipating success rather than hoping for it, he picked up the key ring that afternoon and began his quest immediately. Randall had a thoughtful streak in his otherwise prickly personality: he'd saved Langford the trouble of trying to match each key to the right lock by attaching a card identifying which storeroom or closet in which building it belonged to. Bundled in a sheepskin jacket, a watch cap covering his head, Langford crossed and recrossed the campus in the days ahead, descending gloomy staircases into gloomier basements, all lit by naked bulbs and filled with years of detritus. Broken hammers and screwdrivers, electrical cord and plugs, cardboard boxes, wooden boxes, toolboxes, discarded bookcases, window frames, air conditioners, space heaters, an ironing board or two, screws and nails in plastic boxes on worktables, doorknobs. Doorknobs, but no door.

He returned the ring to Randall, experiencing a letdown proportional to the anticipation with which he'd started.

"Well, if that thing you're looking for is still around, it maybe isn't on the campus. Or maybe it did get thrown out. Sorry I couldn't help you out."

Langford turned to leave, then turned back again. "What's that one old place standing all by itself at the edge of the campus? Faces the arboretum. Looks like a house, a two-story colonial, peeling paint, sign on the door says, 'No Trespassing'?"

"That? Hillsdale House. Oldest building on campus. One of the oldest in town. Goes back to the eighteen thirties. One time it was the home of the school's first president. Wouldn't bother looking in there."

"Why?"

Randall rolled his chair backward and stretched out his heavy legs, crossing his ankles. "Two reasons. Been empty for something like twenty-five years, ain't a thing in it. Second reason, it's in bad shape, dangerous, I'm saying."

"If you're trying to discourage me, you've failed."

"Oh, yeah? Just thought of a third reason. No way in. Doors and windows blocked off or locked, and I don't have a key."

Christmas break started on the eighteenth; the campus was virtually deserted. At around half past seven that night, equipped like a burglar with a prybar, a screwdriver, a lock pick ordered from Amazon, and a headlamp in a carry bag, Langford skirted the Mall, then turned onto a path leading into the arboretum. The tall trees cast shadows in the light of a half-moon. He imagined himself a spy on a clandestine mission. To settle himself down, he sat on a bench facing another and waited until his heartbeat quieted before moving on. A brief walk brought him to the Hillsdale House, as eerie looking as a haunted mansion in the splintered moonlight. For no reason other than instinct, he was certain the object of his quest was inside.

He mounted three stairs to the front porch, its roof supported by wooden pillars blemished by blistered paint. The planks underfoot were sturdy enough when he bounced up and down to test them. Strapping the lamp to his head, he reached up and switched it on and pried loose a two-by-six board nailed across the front door, taking great care not to make any noise or bend the nails too much, as he intended to replace the board once he was done. He bowed slightly to shine the light on the front door handle and the deadbolt above it, inserted a tension tool into the key slot, turned it gently clockwise, as the YouTube video he'd watched had instructed, and inserted the pick, feeling for the tumblers to fall into place. It took him three tries. He turned the handle, put his shoulder to the door; it swung open. Langford stepped inside.

The floor felt spongy in places, probably from dry rot or termites. The headlamp illuminated a hall and a stairway, and he caught in his peripheral vision archways leading to rooms on the right and left, both empty. He searched them and three other rooms but did not find anything.

Making his way back to the entrance, he spotted a door he'd missed. It wasn't gray and white, wasn't *the* door but merely *a* door. He opened it and looked down at stairs leading to a cellar filled with cast-off furniture and lamps and rugs. All manner of junk. Holding onto the door jamb, he placed one foot on the top stair and thumped against it, finding it solid. Something made a scratching noise below. Probably a rat. The air was as stale as the air in a closed cavern. Langford tried the next stair and the next and the next and was about halfway down when the headlamp's beam fell on it, leaning off to one side against a stone cellar wall. Gray and white, the gray so faded it was itself almost white. The door! A manila card, with writing on it, was attached to its dull copper knob by what appeared to be a wire. Ezra's door! Had to be. He started down again and the next stair gave way under his weight, and he pitched forward in a semi-somersault and banged the back of his skull on the dirt floor, packed hard as concrete, and everything went black.

"Congratulations. You just about killed yourself." This time Langford not only heard Pound speaking but saw his tall, lean figure standing over him. Reddish air, eyes deep-set in a gaunt face. Langford wasn't frightened by the apparition; in fact, he was thrilled to behold the great poet.

"What . . . what . . . Can you . . . help me get up?"

"No."

"No?"

"*Capisce inglese*? No has practically universal meaning." Ezra—Langford thought they could now be on a first-name basis—sat down beside him. "One question. You read my essay?"

"*T.P.'s Weekly*?"

"Sure. What did you get out of it?"

Haltingly, Langford related the interpretation he and Amy Wessel had devised.

"Yup," Ezra replied. "That's one possibility. The other is this—Great poets are born great, some aren't. Some are just very good or kind of good or downright lousy, and no matter how hard they work at technique, they'll never be great. Y'know, Hemingway tried to teach me to box."

"Uh-huh."

"I just didn't have it in me. Papa could whip my skinny ass every day and twice on Saturday night."

"My head hurts and I think I'm bleeding." Langford rubbed his injury and displayed blood on his fingertips.

"You'll live," said Ezra. "But you'll never get through your writer's block as long as you keep *trying* to be a goddamn genius, cuz a genius you ain't."

And with that he was gone, vanished as quickly as he'd appeared and Langford called out, "Wait! You can't just . . . Wait! Ezra!"

Langford opened his eyes. He was outside on the porch, strapped to a stretcher and covered with a blanket against the cold. A woman in a uniform was kneeling over him. "He's regained consciousness," she said. He blinked and saw a man standing behind her. He wore the same uniform: blue jacket, a patch on each sleeve. Paramedic. Alongside him stood another man in a different uniform, which Langford recognized as the one worn by the campus police.

"Sir? Can you answer a few questions?" the first man asked.

Langford raised his head slightly and saw red and white roof lights flashing a short distance away, through the arboretum trees.

"Are you able to answer a few questions?" the man repeated.

He gestured that he was.

The paramedic asked his name, age, and if he knew where he was. He responded correctly, but was stumped by the questions that followed: Who is the President of the United States? What year is it? What month?

Do you remember what happened to you?"

"Fell. Guess I fell."

"This man"—motioning at the cop—"was making his rounds when he noticed the door to the house ajar and the plank that had been nailed across it on the porch. He went inside and heard you yelling something in the cellar. He found you and called us."

"Yelling?"

"Sounded like a name," the cop said.

"You may have a concussion," the female paramedic said. "We're going to take you to the ER."

"Yelling what name?"

"We had a tough time hauling you up those rickety stairs," the cop said. "When you're feeling better, you can tell me what you were up to, breaking into this place."

"What name was I yelling?"

"Sounded like Ezra. 'Ezra! Wait!' Something like that. Was somebody else with you?"

Langford thought for a while, not saying anything. His head throbbed but his mind had cleared. Not a genius, and that was all right. What an idiot he'd been to think otherwise.

"No," he replied to the cop. "Nobody."